OUT OF THIS WORLD

By the Author

Dreaming of Her

Under Her Spell

Out of This World

OUT OF THIS WORLD

by

Maggie Morton

A Division of Bold Strokes Books

2014

OUT OF THIS WORLD

ISBN 13: 978-1-62639-083-6

This Trade Paperback Original Is Published By
Bold Strokes Books, Inc.
P.O. Box 249
Valley Falls, NY 12185

First Edition: August 2014

CREDITS
EDITOR: SHELLEY THRASHER
PRODUCTION DESIGN: STACIA SEAMAN
COVER DESIGN BY SHERI (GRAPHICARTIST2020@HOTMAIL.COM)

Acknowledgments

I would like to begin by thanking Shelley for her excellent editing (as per usual). Everyone at Bold Strokes Books deserves many, many kudos as well for running such a great company that I'm delighted to have been published by a third time. I'd also like to praise Sheri for what I think is my best cover yet. And I would like to thank my friend Susan M., for helping me to get much better at seeing which words should go where, and which words shouldn't go anywhere. Finally, I would like to thank Bucko, Beanie, and Bunky for being there for me more than anyone else I know.

To Mr. M., one of the brightest stars in my night sky

CHAPTER ONE

A re you positive I can't get my luggage until a week from now?" Iris was on the verge of tears, or at least she might have been if she hadn't taken a Xanax before she got on the plane. Here she was, her feet finally on foreign soil—her first time out of the United States. It should have been the height of excitement for her, but all she could think about was how Jane would have handled this better than her.

Jane always handled things better than she did. Things like who had been the last one to pay for dinner, how many times they'd had sex that month, what date their tickets for the opera were for, or any number of other important things that never seemed to stick in Iris's head. She knew she wasn't a complete idiot, as teacher after teacher had praised her work in high school and now in college. But apparently, she wasn't smart enough to keep Jane around. Or sexy enough. Or... "something" enough.

Yes, obviously something was wrong with her, or Jane would have stayed with her. Jane wouldn't have dumped her if she were a better, more appealing person. And she definitely wouldn't have dumped her for a man. Jane, the long-term lesbian; Jane, her hopefully permanent partner; Jane, whom Iris had been planning to spend the rest of her life with. But their third anniversary had neared about a year ago, and Jane had started acting stranger and stranger, until she told Iris they were over, and she was leaving her for her lab partner, Billy. Billy. What a stupid name.

"I'm very sorry, miss." The woman at the baggage-claim stand looked so full of fear it almost seemed like she was expecting Iris to hit her. The poor woman probably had to deal with people who were much angrier than she was right then. Iris understood just how thankless jobs like this could be, especially after spending her own fair (unfair?) share of time in the service industry.

"No…no, it's fine." Iris stifled a sigh, one she knew was well-earned, but she also knew it would make this poor woman's night even worse. Not that Iris's was off to a great start. First she had endured the four-hour delay in her departure from New York, and now her luggage was lost, perhaps *permanently*. Just like it seemed as if Jane might be permanently lost. Oh well, at least she still had plenty of baggage left over from her last few months with Jane.

"Really, miss? Are you sure? I could give you a voucher for twenty dollars off your next flight if you'd like."

"Sure. I'd be happy to take it." Iris smiled as warmly as she could manage at the woman behind the counter and was rewarded with a smile that showed how beautiful the woman helping her must have been when she wasn't busy looking so frightened. Iris wasn't all that scary—she'd been incredibly shy her entire life and had just begun to come out of her shell when Jane gave her reasons galore to shimmy right back into it.

The woman reached beneath the counter and handed her two strips of paper. "Here's an extra one, although I'm not supposed to do this," she said in a quiet voice. "You're the nicest person I've helped all day."

Well! The lost baggage came with a slight benefit, then.

Maybe not to Iris, but to this pretty woman. "Thanks," she said, in as soft a voice as the woman had used. Soft because that was her usual speaking voice. She was trying to draw herself *back* out of her shell by going on this trip, at her therapist's suggestion. She had been terrified when Uma, her therapist, had recommended her trip, and Uma had told her that was all the more reason to go. "The things that scare us are sometimes the best medicine when we're going through rough times."

So here she was, in Amsterdam, with no luggage other than her carry-on, no idea where she was staying (because all of that information had been in her luggage), and two twenty-dollar vouchers. Maybe they would be enough for a flight home, she joked to herself, coming very close to deciding to use them that very night. She was exhausted, hungry, and getting scared about how the rest of her ten-day trip would go, considering how badly it had started out.

"Um, could you tell me where the nearest taxis are?" she asked the woman.

"To the right and down the next two hallways. You'll go over one of those moving walkways, and then you'll see many doors. Go through any of them."

The woman spoke with an unrecognizable accent, but her English was much more impressive than Iris's ability with any language other than her own.

"Thanks," she said again, tucking the two vouchers into her bag. Then she turned and started walking to her right, careful to not make eye contact with any of the men nearby. She didn't want any unwanted attention while she was here. She didn't want any attention period, or at least any beyond the "attention" she'd decided to look for here when she'd bought her ticket. Maybe it was the Xanax speaking, or maybe it was just that it had been almost a year, but she wasn't going to let her normally hesitant nature stop her on this trip. She hadn't just come here for the food, and of course she hadn't come for the drugs. Nope, she'd chosen this particular city for one thing and one thing alone: she'd come here to get laid.

The airport employee's directions proved to be accurate, and a taxi was waiting right outside the first set of doors Iris walked through. She climbed into the cab and got ready to tell the taxi driver where she wanted to go, but before she could, he started driving. And then the strangest thing happened—an immensely strong wave of exhaustion crashed over her, and within seconds, Iris was fast asleep.

❖

She woke up what could have been either minutes or hours later. Or even days. But she didn't see any clocks nearby to tell her how long it'd been, and the mattress she was lying on was lumpy and uneven. As she opened her eyes, her memories came shooting back into her head. The lost luggage. The taxi she'd gotten into. And how she'd fallen asleep as soon as the driver had taken off.

"Fuck!" Iris leapt up. She was standing under a starry, full-mooned sky, in a giant field, and she had absolutely no idea where she was. "What to do, w-what to do…" she stammered, glancing left and right. On the ground a few feet away lay her bag, and she rushed over to it. Maybe she could call her mom, or her brother, and get their help. But after she'd scrambled to her bag and dumped its contents out onto the ground, she realized quite quickly that not only was she in the middle of nowhere with no idea where she was, but she also had no phone, no wallet, and nothing except the magazine she'd read on the flight, her diary, two pens, and the airplane vouchers. A lot of good *those* would do now.

What was she supposed to do in this predicament? Then a bit of her therapist's advice came back to her. Uma had told her to take three deep breaths and picture herself in a special place whenever she started to get tense. So Iris did this now, shutting her eyes and visualizing herself in a hammock on a beach, with two gorgeous women fanning her with palm fronds. And then she added the thought that the two women were naked because, hell, it couldn't hurt. And why not make them lay down a blanket and undress her, and start…

"Damn it." Yes, it'd been far too long since she'd had sex, because here she was, lost and without any way to get *un*-lost, and she was fantasizing. The fantasy, though, had seemed to clear her head, because as she opened her eyes, she felt at least a little calmer.

With the small bit of calm she'd managed to generate with her fantasy, she could take in her surroundings a bit better. About fifty feet to her left stood a large domed structure, which looked ancient. She might as well check it out. Perhaps she'd find some sort of ancient communication device in it, too. So she quickly stuffed everything back into her bag and walked the short distance to the building's entrance.

Once inside, she observed what little she could with the moon's light coming through mid-sized openings in its circular, single wall. There seemed to be some kind of art on it. Squinting to make it out, she walked a little closer to one of the walls and felt the ground begin to shake slightly. So Holland had earthquakes, apparently, and she was here just in time to experience one. If she was even *in* Holland. Iris might have started wondering again if she'd ever see her home again; Iris might have started to worry she'd never see anyone she loved ever again; and while she was at it, Iris might have started worrying that she'd never get to have sex again. All of these worries would possibly have occurred to her if the floor hadn't cracked and then collapsed, causing her to scream as she fell into the darkness below.

She dropped for what seemed like ages, all the while screaming the loudest she probably ever had. And then, just as suddenly as the falling had started, it stopped, as she landed with a small thudding noise on top of something that made a sound somewhat like *Oof!* This something, whatever it was, looked like the sky had before she'd started falling, except she could see no moon, and the stars only covered a small bit of space beneath her.

"You can stop screaming now," the sky said, and then she felt the sky reaching out to her right.

The shock of sudden brightness all around her forced her to shut her eyes, and she slowly reopened them as they adjusted to the light. She was in a room, made out of wide wooden slats, with a kitchen, a table and several chairs, and a small, blanketed bed that she happened to be on top of. The room's light was coming from a small kerosene lamp on the table to her right. But its flame didn't look quite normal to Iris. Not that any of this looked—or seemed—normal.

"So, how did you get here, pretty lady?" It was the same voice that had spoken before, and so the last thing Iris noticed about the room she was in was that it held a beautiful, pitch-black-skinned woman, with tiny, twinkling lights spread across her skin. Apparently, the night sky she'd fallen on was a woman, with some amazingly rendered tattoos. And this tattooed woman, with kissable, shimmery white lips and short, messy white hair, happened to think she was pretty.

"Me?" Iris squeaked.

"Who else do you see in this room, other than you and me?"

Iris couldn't help it—she started to giggle, giggles that

turned into loud laughs, laughs that would have gone on for a long time if the woman hadn't interrupted them with the words, "Well, wherever you've come from, and whatever you're laughing about, I don't care to find out right away. Instead, will you let me kiss you?"

Right then Iris realized the woman was naked, each of her erect nipples matching the color of her lips and peeking out from underneath the bed's blanket.

Iris wouldn't have normally responded the way she did to this woman's words, but now, after she'd lost her luggage, her way, and, seemingly, her mind, she couldn't deny it. She was horny as hell, she had a sexy, naked goddess beneath her, and the mere suggestion of a kiss had her cunt throbbing in a way it never had before.

"Yes, go ahead," she murmured, and the star-covered, naked woman placed her hand on Iris's cheek and kissed her.

Iris melted as soon as the woman's lips touched hers, the heat that had begun in her thighs and crotch now spreading throughout her entire body. It seemed as if the heat was going to travel to every place the woman touched her. One of her ebony, star-flecked hands caressed Iris's shoulder first, then drifted over to her collarbone, where the woman traced it with the backs of her fingers, sending a slight shiver down Iris's back.

"I feel underdressed," the woman whispered across Iris's lips. "Why don't you help me to feel more comfortable by taking off some of your copious amount of skin-covering material?"

"My...my clothes, you mean?" Iris glanced down at what she was wearing—a loose, thigh-length T-shirt and gray slacks. Her shoes were even still on. "I'm sorry," she told the woman as soon as she realized this. "I definitely shouldn't have my shoes on your bed. Just give me a moment."

"I'll give you a moment, but not much longer. I'm dying to see if your body is as delectable as your face and hair."

Delectable? Me?

Iris noticed a mirror to the left of the bed now and took a moment to see if she looked any better than usual. Her chin-length, straight brown hair was messier than she liked it to be, probably from sleeping in that field, and her makeup was completely gone, although her parted lips looked pinker than usual, and her cheeks were flushed in a nice way, too, probably from her current arousal.

"Stop admiring your attractive face and show me your body, whatever your name is."

"Iris. It's Iris," she answered, turning away from the mirror and back toward the woman.

As she pulled her T-shirt over her head, she heard the woman say, "My name is Anandra. I can truthfully say it is far more than a pleasure to meet you, or it will be once you press your naked skin against mine. It's been much too long since I've given myself over to another woman's body. Almost three weeks, if my count is right."

"Three weeks?" Iris whispered. "How about a *year?*"

"What was that?" Anandra asked, now back in view, as Iris's T-shirt hit the floor. She made quick work of taking off her bra, and then she slipped out of her shoes and stripped off her pants and panties. Now she was just as naked as the woman before her, if not more, because she might possibly be wearing some underwear on her lower half, all of it still hidden beneath the bed's covers. Luckily for Iris, she was just about to find out.

This woman, this Anandra, made her mouth water like it hadn't in a year. Or maybe longer, because her hunger for Anandra was too strong to fight. Not that she wanted to, not in the least. This may have been a very strange situation, but she'd never seen a woman as tasty-looking as this one, and if she was lucky enough to be wanted by her, there wasn't a chance in hell Iris would refuse her advances.

"Come here and get under the covers. I want you to warm me up and make me wet."

Iris began to walk back over to the bed; as she did, the woman continued to talk in a low, calm voice, sounding sure of her control over Iris, a certainty that was well-earned. "I want you to make me quiver with need. I want you to draw sounds out of me the likes of which I've never made before. I want you to make me shake like the earth, cry out like the wind, and crash into orgasm like giant waves across the shore. Are you ready to please me in all these ways?"

Iris had slid under the covers while Anandra spoke, and she was more than ready, but instead of answering the woman with her voice, she placed her lips around one of Anandra's perfect, star-like nipples and began to suck, drawing a small moan from between the woman's lips. "Mmm, that's just what I needed, Iris." She paused to moan again, then continued. "But it's just the beginning of what I desire from you."

"I'm more than happy to give you more," Iris told her, surprised at her out-of-nowhere boldness around this stranger. She'd never been this way with Jane, always just going along with whatever flow Jane set into motion. Once, Jane had asked her if she even enjoyed sex, and Iris hadn't known what to say.

Well, these first few minutes with Anandra gave her an answer to that question, a very loud and very clear answer: Yes, she did! And her enjoyment grew as Anandra threaded her fingers through Iris's hair and held her in place, her hold gentle but firm. "You should know that I like to be in control, Iris, but I want you to enjoy me controlling you, so stop for a second and decide whether you'd like to give me your permission to be the one who tells you what to do." She let go of Iris's hair and Iris tilted her head up, looking into the woman's now-serious stare. "If at any point it gets to be too much, say the word 'roof,' because I don't want you to do any more falling tonight, unless it's falling into an orgasm or two."

Iris paused for a moment, breaking eye contact and looking down at Anandra's left shoulder. It almost seemed to have been shaped by some sort of higher being, just like the rest of Anandra. How had this jaw-dropping sight of a woman managed to find her interesting and appealing? More than merely "appealing," actually, Iris gathered. She must have found her arousing, perhaps even highly arousing. Iris snapped back from her thoughts and gave Anandra her answer, one she meant and felt. "I want you to control me. I've...I have to be honest. I've never done anything like this before, but I really, really want to. I, um, I almost feel like I *need* to, actually."

"I am happy to fulfill wants as well as needs, but it will be mine we'll be addressing. You may be allowed to come should you please me enough, Iris, but only if you do exactly as I say. Now, return your mouth to my nipple. That's an order."

Iris was happy to do as she'd asked...no, she reminded herself, as she'd *ordered*. She parted her lips and returned her mouth to Anandra's hard nipple, sucking it and flicking her tongue back and forth across its erect surface. After just a few seconds, Anandra returned her hand to Iris's head, gripping a handful of her hair and shoving Iris's face down—hard—against her breast. The action spread Iris's mouth wide, and Anandra's flesh made a gag of sorts now, her mouth stuffed full of nipple and breast. "For future reference," Anandra said, her tone cold and tough, "if your mouth is ever full and you desire to stop, just thump your hand down three times. And if your hands are restrained, just grunt three times."

But instead of grunting, Iris moaned because, using her

free hand, Anandra was now gently tugging one of Iris's nipples. "Keep sucking, keep pleasuring me, and try not to be too startled."

Iris barely had time to wonder what she meant by "startled," because almost instantly the answer came in the form of a quick, rough pinch on Iris's nipple. She grunted and shuddered, pulling back a little from the sudden pain.

"Relax into it, relax and breathe. You'll get used to it after a while."

So Iris did as she was told, allowing her drool to pool around the edges of her mouth while Anandra continued to pinch her poor, inexperienced nipple. Inexperienced to pain, at least, but that lack of experience seemed to be over now. And so did her dislike of the pain, because as Anandra's grasp on her nipple tightened, her body loosened as she relaxed into the pain, and then she started to enjoy it.

She could tell she was enjoying it by the way her cunt was communicating with her, by the way it had grown twice as wet as it had been before her nipple began to be pinched. As she adjusted to the intensity of the sensation, she found she had the ability to take up pleasuring Anandra again, so she began to suck her breast, to move her tongue against her nipple as well as she possibly could. She had a strong urge now to please this woman, and she waited eagerly for whatever Anandra's next directions might be.

"Ah, you've adjusted fast. You must have played like this before."

"Mmm-mmm," Iris grunted around Anandra's breast.

"No? Was that a 'no'? I must admit, I'm surprised, considering how quickly you became comfortable with the pain."

So that was quickly? Iris had felt she had taken some time, but she realized then that it had probably been only a few seconds, the shock of the pain just making time seem to slow down. As she realized this, she also realized that she wanted their time to slow down just as much as it had from Anandra's pinch. She was shocked, though, at how much the pain and control were turning her on. What else had she been missing during her one and only sexual relationship? Were even better things in store for her on this night?

She'd almost entirely forgotten about the incredible shock coming here had caused when she'd suddenly fallen through the floor of the ruins. But all of that could wait until later. She thought to her predicament one last time. Because just after that thought, Anandra yanked Iris away from her breast by her hair, the sharp tension from Anandra's grip against her scalp sending tingles tumbling down her neck and back.

Anandra pulled her head back at a sharp angle and ran her tongue up the side of Iris's neck. Then came her second shock of the night, at least in terms of sexual ones. Anandra cupped her face in one hand, staring into her eyes. "Keep your eyes open and looking into mine," she ordered. And then Iris half grunted, half gasped as Anandra's open palm slapped her across her right cheek.

"Holy fuck!" she cried out, her whole body tightening again at the impact. But she had no way to turn away from the pain, nor a way to change her position, because Anandra was holding her in place on the pillow.

"Was that too much for you?" she asked Iris, and looked concerned for the first time that night.

Iris didn't even need to think before she answered—she knew it in her bones that it wasn't. "No, no," she said, her voice coming out breathy and higher than usual. "No, that was just…exactly…right."

"You *do* like it this way, then. Good. It's been even longer than those three weeks since I fell into bed with a woman who wanted to take what I wanted to give. It's been boring old oral sex and the like for at least two sun-cycles. It was a not-so-small shock to have you land on me like that, but I've seen far stranger things than a woman—a very, very sexy one, at that—falling through my roof in the middle of the night. Now how that happened, that's—"

"I know I probably shouldn't interrupt," Iris said, some of her shyness returning as she spoke, "but I want you to continue."

"Beg, then. Beg me to continue." Anandra tightened her grip on Iris's hair, pulling it tighter and tighter until her back began to bow. "Beg for me to let you please me, to let you taste me, to let you place your tongue on my cunt and get it even wetter than you've made it so far."

"Please," Iris said to her, because she was happy to beg, much more than merely interested in tasting Anandra's cunt. She felt almost like she was desperate to do so. "Please, Anandra, I want to taste you, I want to see what you taste like, I want to get you off, as many times as I can, and I want to be allowed to come when you've had enough."

"That could be arranged. You can get off, I suppose, if you do a good enough job, my little slut." Anandra let go of her hair and slowly pushed Iris's head down her body, and Iris took this chance to kiss her everywhere she could. Anandra was already moaning a bit when Iris's mouth reached her bush, and when Iris pushed her legs apart and brought her lips to the woman's cunt and clit, it seemed like only a couple of minutes passed before Anandra was arching her back, then bucking, and then screaming and clenching the sheets as she came.

Iris kept right on going, though, leading her into a second orgasm and then a third. She was amazed at how easily Anandra came. Not just amazed—she was also kind of jealous. It usually took Iris a good twenty minutes to get off, and she wasn't exactly a screamer, either. But she was still enjoying herself (that was for damn sure!) because she'd never had this kind of effect on her ex. Not even once. Maybe she wasn't as bad in bed as she'd thought.

"S...stop, Iris."

She jerked her head up. "Am I doing something wrong?"

"Oh no, my dear, not a thing. Not...a...thing. It's just that I usually stop after four orgasms at the most, and I think that was five. No, six? I kind of lost count." Anandra's voice sounded relaxed and sated. Iris did as she'd asked, even though she wanted to keep going. Not that she knew what it was like to have too many orgasms. Jane had told her that she took so long to come she was only up for giving Iris one each time they had sex. She'd never complained, but Iris realized now that maybe she should have.

Now she was looking into Anandra's eyes again, her head a few inches above her new partner's. Anandra's beautiful face was flecked with tiny drops of sweat, and Iris got a better look at her now. Her star tattoos suddenly didn't look so much like tattoos. Iris would have to ask her how her tattoo artist had done such realistic work, but first—"Did I do a good enough job to get a turn?"

"Oh, yes, you did!" Anandra grinned, made a small growling noise, and flipped Iris onto her back.

"Wow, you're really strong!" Iris gasped.

"There are many things that I am 'really,' as you're just about to find out."

One of those "many things" she also was "really" proved to be "good in bed," because apparently Iris's usual twenty minutes could be shortened to ten, at least if Anandra's mouth was involved. With her pleasure ramping up at a much faster pace than in the past, Iris showed her shock with many, many noises and sounds, the likes of which she'd never made before.

After she came, she took a few deep breaths and said, "How... didya...did you...do...you know? That?"

"Oh," Anandra said, lifting her head from Iris's cunt with the expression of the dyke who ate the pussy, "there's much more where that came from. If you'd care for me to continue, that is?"

"Yes! Yes, please!"

Soon, Iris was pleading for a break, and so Anandra kissed her once on her still rather sensitized clit and then lay down next to her. "I've got to get back to sleep now. I have a lot to do tomorrow."

Iris realized then how tired she was, between the lack of sleep on her cross-oceanic flight and the whole falling-through-a-floor-in-the-middle-of-nowhere thing. And the amazing, best-of-her-life sex. But... "I'm really tired," she told Anandra, "too tired to figure all this out. Can I crash in your bed? I'm guessing that in the morning I'll either wake up in my hotel in Amsterdam and realize this was all a very nice dream...well, mostly nice...or I'll wake up here and have to start making sense of all of this...this..."

"Sounds good to me," Anandra mumbled, shutting off her lamp.

Iris got as comfortable as she could under the covers. She wasn't used to sleeping in the buff, but then again, when she'd boarded that plane out of the country she'd decided it was time for some changes. And whether this was a nice—but strange—dream, or whether it was really happening, she'd have to wait until the morning to discover the truth.

She found Anandra's quiet snores strangely soothing and drifted off to sleep about as quickly as she'd gotten off the first time.

❖

A sound woke Iris up from a relatively deep slumber. She'd been dreaming about a threesome with two ladies of the night—two quite lovely and skilled ones, at that—and so she wasn't exactly happy to be awakened. It took her a few seconds to get her bearings, the dim light from Anandra's tattoos reminding her of where she was. She admitted to herself in that moment that tattoos didn't usually glow in the dark, and they *definitely* didn't twinkle. That old children's song about twinkling stars came to mind then, and she started humming it softly.

"No, sir, I do *not* want you to buy me new feet," Anandra mumbled, "for mine still smell fine to me." She was clearly still deep asleep, because she snorted softly and then rolled over, flopping an arm over Iris's waist.

Iris wanted to close her eyes and go back to sleep, but something was unsettling about the bedroom she was in right then; something about it wasn't quite right. Then she heard a small noise from her left. It sounded like a sigh. Iris whipped her head around and saw a petite, dark figure standing there. It might have been human-shaped, but that didn't stop it from scaring the breath out of her. She opened her mouth and got ready to scream.

Chapter Two

G ood morning, lazy limbs. Do you want to get up, or are you planning to sleep all the way through sunrise?"

Iris had made it a proud habit of always sleeping through sunrise. Besides, none of her classes started until nine at the earliest. "Jane," she told the person speaking, rubbing her eyes, "you know I never, ever, *ever* get up this early."

But it wasn't Jane standing in front of her, reaching down and waving a sweet-smelling piece of fruit under her nose. It wasn't only the fruit that didn't look familiar—dark blue and oval with small pink seeds. The woman in front of her, with black skin and little pale flecks across it that all put off a slight light, was smiling wryly, almost looking proud of herself for insulting Iris's morning-rising habits.

"You're...you're not Jane. You're Anandra. You're...it was all *real?*" Iris threw back the covers and got to her feet, her legs shaky and now covered in goose bumps from the early morning cold. "And I never, ever get up this early. Not without a very good reason and some very good coffee."

"I don't know what this 'coffee' stuff is," Anandra said, handing her the fruit, "but you do have a very good reason to get up. I'm leaving when the sun is just a little higher in the sky, and I'm guessing you'll want to go with me."

"Go with you? Where?" Iris rubbed her chilly arms and shivered, suddenly finding the time to realize she was naked. "Just a second. I should probably put some clothes on, first."

"Yours were covered in dirt. I don't have time to go to the village washer's, so you'll have to borrow some of mine. You look like you're about the same size as me. I laid them out in the chair by your side of the bed." Anandra gestured toward the chair with a large, pearl-handled knife that held the other half of the fruit. She took a large bite of its juicy-looking flesh and sat down at a small square table a few feet from the foot of the bed.

"Village washer? You mean, the Laundromat?"

"That must be what you call the washer's home in your world. I'm guessing next you'll be telling me you've never heard of magic, and then you'll tell me that—"

"Magic?" Anandra was right: her clothes were caked with dirt, totally unwearable. Hopefully she was also right about the two of them being the same size. "Why did you bring up magic?" She put on the soft black panties sitting on top of the pile of clothes, then slid into the brown leather pants that had been beneath them. "I know what magic is, of course," she said. "David Copperfield, Penn and Teller, et cetera."

"Those must be the best magic makers of your land. I know of only a few other magic makers, like Selehn and my magic tutor, Nerec."

"Wait…a…minute." Iris didn't mean this literally, but she did have to make Anandra wait a minute, because she wouldn't be able to talk while she put on the light-brown woven tank that had been beneath the pants. It showed off just a touch of cleavage from the top of her breasts, hers clearly a cup size or so bigger than Anandra's, who wore an identical shirt without, sadly, a single bit of her yummy breasts showing over the top.

But she had more important things to figure out than a way to get Anandra back out of her clothes. That would have to come later. First, she wanted to find out where she was. And why, if she'd heard her right, Anandra had asked her what a "minute" was while she was pulling the shirt over her head.

"I like your underthings," Anandra told her with a sexy smile. "Your tailor must have a lot of skill to do such exceptional work. I might like to see them in my hands later tonight. And I'd like to see the rest of you in my hands then, as well."

"I'd like that, too. But first I'd like to know where I am. And why it looks like I'm up in the sky. And why you keep talking about magic."

"You seem to have heard of magic, and yet it sounds like you don't know much about it. Maybe magic is different in your land?"

Iris sat down on a small stool that had been pulled up to the table. At her spot lay a large plate filled with food and a tall earthenware mug filled to the brim with something that looked and smelled a lot like coffee. "Thank God, at least there's coffee here." She took a large gulp of what had long been her very favorite caffeinated beverage. It was amazing as coffee went, but something was off about its flavor. It tasted only slightly like coffee, Iris realized with a second swallow.

"This coffee is really good. Amsterdam isn't famous for its coffee, at least that I know of. Is that where I am? Holland?" She took another swallow, then dug into her food. There were eggs, a piece of whole-wheat bread coated in jam, and two slices of ham, which also surprised her by not tasting quite right when she took a bite.

"That's not coffee, Iris, it's cheefen. And you're not in Amsterdam, wherever that is. You're in the Basthar territory, of course, and this is my tree-home. I'd give you a warmer welcome, introduce you around, but we need to leave soon. I have an urgent message to deliver to the Queen, after all. Which reminds me…" At those words, Anandra pulled a jar off a shelf by the room's smaller window and uncorked it. She sprinkled some white powder from the jar into her palm and dumped it onto the table. Iris heard a quiet *whoosh*, and then a small box appeared on the table. "Is this the same as the magic in your land?" Anandra asked her.

Iris was having a hard time swallowing her last bite of bread. She began to cough and took a few long gulps of her coffee…or cheefen…or what*ever* the fuck it was. "I'm still on Earth, right?" she asked when she could breathe again. "This is just some kind of candid-camera thing. Next my therapist will come waltzing into the room, telling me this was all a plan to shake me out of my funk and get me out of my shell, or at least back to normal. Well, as hot as the sex was, and as nice as you're being to me, I'm ready to find out what's *really* going on. Could you please, please tell me?"

"What's really going on is just what I told you," Anandra said, opening the box and taking out a wax-sealed roll of parchment. "Here is the message for the Queen. I've also come to think that you don't seem to know what magic is, not at all. Nor are you in this 'Earth' place you mentioned. Not right now, at least." She spread her arms wide. "Welcome to my land, Iris. Welcome to Oria."

At those words, Iris did something for the first time in many, many years, something that had thoroughly embarrassed her each of the five times it had previously occurred: she fainted.

When she came to, not much about her circumstances had changed, other than the fact that she was back on the bed she'd slept on, and her face was being fanned by her notebook, which was floating in the air above her face. Iris realized something then, as she watched the levitating paisley notebook flop from side to side: she could either do her best to accept all of this, or she could let it drive her mad—if she wasn't mad already.

Maybe her newfound sexual prowess had gone to her head, or maybe she'd finally had it with always being hesitant, and shy, and scared, which were things Jane had often told her she needed to work on. Or maybe it was just that she felt she had no choice. Whatever it was, her head was much clearer when she lifted it off the pillows before she got to her feet. She seemed to be more aware than she had been in months. "Let's do it, then," she told Anandra. "Take me to the castle."

"Sounds like a plan. And speaking of plans, my tutor might have a way to help you get home. As I said, he's incredibly skilled with potions and powders, and his specialty is scrolls. Which are probably the only things powerful enough to get you back to wherever this Earth place is located. I should warn you, though." Anandra rose from the bed and grabbed the notebook out of the air, handing it to Iris. "This trip will not be without risk. Our land has its fair share of dangers. I am a very skilled fighter, if I do say so myself, and I am quite good with a dagger, so I will do my best to protect you. My sack should come in handy as well," she said, pointing to a small leather satchel sitting near the room's only door. "It is practically bottomless, after all, and most of the time it proves to be very helpful. Lastly, at the very least, it will take us three full days to get to the castle, and that is if everything works out in our favor. In my life, it doesn't tend to. I can't yet speak for yours."

Iris watched as she picked up a large silver dagger, slipped it into a sheath, and buckled it to her left thigh. "That's a scary-looking knife," she remarked.

"I hope it is, for our sake. If everyone thinks it looks scary enough, we won't come across any problems on our trip. Ha! As if *that's* likely."

"You keep talking about how dangerous it'll be. Will we encounter other people with magical abilities on the way there?"

"Most likely many. And magical beings as well. They're the real ones to watch out for, since you can't see them getting ready to perform their enchantments or cast their spells. They have no need for potions or powders, nor do they need scrolls to cast a spell."

"Scrolls? What are those? And how do they work?"

"Scrolls?" Anandra tossed Iris her bag and notebook, which she surprised herself by catching. "They're just like the potions and powders and other magically imbued items you can buy from sellers. They came into being many centuries ago, from our forefathers and foremothers, the first magical people of our land."

"And?" Iris gestured at Anandra in hopes she'd tell her more, but Anandra shook her head.

"I don't know how much about magic I should be telling you right now. I am not a tutor like Nerec, and that's what you really need. Maybe it will be explained along the way, but right now, the most important thing is that we get going." She pushed her chair under the table and went over to the sink with their breakfast dishes, giving each of them a quick rinse. "Don't want any moldy plates to return home to. Or any scavengers staying near my house in hopes of more delicious bread and jam." She dried her hands on a towel by the sink, then sprinkled some more powder over the message for the Queen, and Iris was about ten percent less shocked this time when it became invisible again. Anandra acted like she was placing it in her bag—Iris couldn't even know for sure whether it was actually in her hand—and then she slung the bag over her shoulder and gestured toward the door. "Ladies second. Submissives, too. I don't want you to slip and fall on your way down, after all."

She opened the narrow, fur-covered door, revealing a small deck and what looked like the tops of at least three trees. Each was about ten feet away from the room they were in, and each held a small circular building the same color as the tree it sat in. How high up were they? Iris wondered.

"I hope you're not afraid of heights," Anandra told her, and then she kicked something off the deck and disappeared over its edge.

"What the…" Where had she gone? She couldn't have just jumped to her death, that much seemed somewhat obvious. So Iris slipped her notebook into her bag, zipped it up, and walked through the doorway. With hesitant steps, because she was more than a little afraid of heights, she walked up to where Anandra had just been standing and looked over the deck's edge.

No, she hadn't jumped to her death. Instead, Anandra was quickly descending a rope ladder hanging between the deck and the frighteningly far-away ground. Iris shuddered a little as she estimated that they must have been at least fifty feet up in the air. She didn't have much choice, though, so she shut the front door and, as carefully and as slowly as she could, swung herself over the edge and began climbing down. Much slower than her clearly climbing-skilled new acquaintance.

And new lover. She couldn't help imagining their previous night's escapades…the surprising pain…and her surprising enjoyment of it. It had been more than just enjoyment, she realized as she climbed, because it had awakened her libido in a way Jane had never been able to. This realization didn't make that much of a difference in how she felt about their breakup, though. She still wanted Jane back, and it was that sad thought and a train of connected ones that kept her mind busy on her way down, mercifully washing away any thoughts of how far she had to fall.

When her feet met the forest floor, she was happy that her arms and legs hurt only a little. Apparently exercising regularly throughout her newly single year had been worth it, at least for these last few minutes. She was even a little proud of herself for getting down as fast as she had. But then she turned and saw Anandra, tapping her foot and clearly impatient. Well, it wasn't like Iris got that many chances to climb up and down fifty-foot long rope ladders in *her* world.

"You ready, then?"

"As ready as I'll ever be," Iris said. Like a human could be ready to face a treacherous trek through this unknown, magic-filled world. What might they come across as they walked? Monsters? Demons? Fairies? And why hadn't this world caught on to the internal-combustion engine the way hers had?

"Why don't you have a horse? Or a donkey, or something, to help you travel faster?" she asked as they began to walk along a path through the tall trees. Only small patches of the early morning sun managed to reach all the way down through the trees to their path, but they had more than enough light to see by as they went along the wide forest trail.

"Oh, I prefer to travel on foot. Always have."

Iris made a few more attempts at conversation, but Anandra seemed content to just walk and breathe and be quiet, so she gave up and tried to enjoy taking in her surroundings. It was only then that she thought to look at her wristwatch, to see what time it was back on Earth, but of course, that seemed to have been yet another item taken by whoever had left her in that field.

"If you're looking for your strange bracelet, I put it in your bag. It was far too conspicuous for a trip such as ours, and it would have made us stand out."

"Ah. Thanks for not throwing it out your window, then."

"I thought it could possibly come in handy at some point. Besides, if I threw away your things, you might not want to sleep with me again." Anandra smiled and gave her a small nudge. "We wouldn't want that now, would we?"

"No, not at all!" Good, so there *would* be a repeat performance of the night before. Hopefully soon, Iris thought, because—

And Anandra seemed to think soon would be good, too, because she placed her hands on Iris's hips and kissed her, this time nipping a little at Iris's bottom lip as she thrust her tongue into her mouth. Iris's cunt grew warm as they kissed, and she wished they'd had more time before they left, time for a second go at it. But maybe wherever they stayed that night, they could "go" that second time upon their arrival.

Just as suddenly as Anandra had started kissing her, she stopped. "It's time to walk, now. We'll have time for play tonight, when we reach my friends' home." She smacked Iris's ass—quite hard, at that—and started down the path once more.

They settled into silence again, but this time Iris minded it less, because she had all kinds of dirty thoughts to keep her company now, thoughts about what they might do that night when they reached wherever they'd be staying. Nightfall couldn't come soon enough, Iris decided, and neither could she.

CHAPTER THREE

What must have been at least a few hours later, they finally reached the edge of the woods. Just beyond was a stretch of low, healthy-looking grass, and a bit farther along was a mid-sized, dark-green river. Iris could have sat in front of it all day, with perhaps some swimming every few hours or so, but then a sudden movement near the closest bank made her fantasy much less appealing.

A gigantic, brown alligator sat there, sunning itself and singing somewhat operatically. Iris wasn't used to running across giant singing alligators when she went walking, so she just did what came naturally and froze in place. Anandra had frozen, too, but not before she'd pulled out her knife and taken a defensive stance. When she noticed Iris looking at her, she put her finger to her lips and then made a series of gestures, like the ones SWAT teams always made in rescue films. Iris, of course, had no idea whatsoever what they meant, so she decided to continue staying immobile for as long as she could.

But it was too late. The alligator had stopped singing and was starting in their direction. As it waddled closer and closer, Iris grew more and more scared. Was she about to become lunch for someone else before she'd even had a chance to have her own?

"Get behind me," Anandra ordered sotto voce. It wasn't the kind of order she'd been imagining her giving for the last hour, but Iris wasn't about to complain. She hurried behind Anandra and got ready to become food, shutting her eyes tight. Then she just listened.

First she heard a loud smacking sound. Then a few grunts: one sounded like it came from Anandra, and the other was lower pitched, just like the alligator's singing voice. Then a high-pitched scream, and finally, what sounded like a boulder hitting the ground and then what might have been the feet of something large moving away from them at high speed.

"You can open your eyes now, you big bowl of pudding. She's leaving."

Iris did as Anandra said and saw that her companion was the clear victor in the fight. The alligator had, so to speak, turned tail and run, as it had just reached the water and started swimming away from them. "What did you *do*?" Iris asked.

"Oh, just showed her that she'd be better off sticking to singing rather than fighting." Iris noticed then that Anandra's dagger had a few flecks of red on it, red that Anandra wiped on the grass before putting it away. "I told you, by the way."

"Told me what?" Iris asked, following Anandra along the river and toward a patch of much-taller grass.

"I told you risk would be involved. Good thing you have me along, huh?"

"Yeah, can't say I'm not grateful." *In more ways than one.*

Just as they reached a stretch of high grass, Anandra stopped and bent down, pulling two large lavender-colored flowers from their stalks. She handed them to Iris and picked two more. "Ball those up and put them in your ears."

"*What?*"

"You'll thank me later. The magical beings in this field

can enchant you with their words, and you'll never want to leave this place if you hear them clearly. These flowers are the best defense against them you'll get."

"Whatever you say." Iris rolled each flower into a tight ball and pushed each one gently into her ear canals. Hopefully Anandra wasn't just doing some kind of hazing experiment on her: let's see what all we can trick the naïve human into doing!

Only a few steps into the taller-than-her-head grasses, Iris began to hear some loud rustling coming from far away. It had been a little windy by the river, so naturally, it had to be the wind. That was what she told herself at least, until she saw Anandra draw her knife and pull back her arm, sending the knife whizzing through the grass at an impossibly high speed. No human could have thrown something that hard, she thought, but Anandra clearly wasn't human. A distant cry of pain managed to make its way through the flowers in Iris's ears, and then she watched as Anandra took off in the same direction she'd just thrown her knife. Iris only paused for a second before she started running, but she could barely keep up and was panting hard by the time she got to Anandra.

She was leaning over a man, curled into a ball, and clearly he was no longer alive. "You killed someone?" Iris yelled at her, and she was more than ready to yell some more.

"Just wait one small while."

Before Iris's very eyes, the man changed shape, into that of a white deer with a thin line of green fluid running down its neck. "I have just the thing for this," Anandra told her, reaching her hand and then her arm into her leather satchel. She withdrew a small black bottle and unscrewed the lid. Attached to the lid was a dropper, and she let three drops of clear liquid fall onto the animal's side. "You see," Anandra said, as the creature began to shrink and change color, "not only are these creatures deadly, able to lure people and other beings to their deaths, but they're also full of magic. I gained some of my skill with the knife from eating one of these creatures, and now I want you to do the same. It may not work, since you're from another world, but it's still worth a try."

The creature continued to shrink and change color, until in its place lay a large, heavily marbled steak, just like the ones Iris's adoptive mom Jackie used to buy at the grocery store. Anandra picked it up off the ground and put it in her bag. "Let's get the rest of the way through the grasses, and then we can find a good spot to have lunch. I'd say we've earned it!"

Iris couldn't even come close to disagreeing. She hadn't experienced this much excitement since…well, never. "I'm pretty hungry, actually. What did you bring for lunch?"

"I'll be having some bread and hard cheese, unlike you. Remember, you have a steak to eat."

"Isn't that a little heavy for lunch?" Iris mumbled as they went through the high grass. Every now and then Anandra used her knife to chop through a few stalks of the tall vegetation, but most of the time, their path was unobstructed. Now Iris was wondering something, so she asked, "Do you pass through this field often?"

"Not if I can help it!" Anandra said with a laugh.

After what seemed like far too long to a rather hungry Iris and her growling stomach, they reached the end of the field. Anandra put her sack down next to a short tree with peeling red bark and similarly colored leaves. It reminded Iris of the manzanita trees of her world.

"What's this tree called?" She sat down beside Anandra, watching as she reached into her bag and pulled out a small grate and what looked like a well-crafted, small barbecue with three legs and white markings around its bowl. Iris forgot she'd asked a question as, next, Anandra blew over the top of the bowl and flames began to peek out over its top. "That's not how we make fire in my world."

"How do you make it there?" Anandra took the steak out of the bag and placed it on top of the grate, settling herself on the ground behind it. Next she took out some tongs, and Iris began to wonder exactly how much that bag of hers actually held. It had already been impressive enough to her when the barbecue had come out of the barely big enough opening at its top. But Iris knew by now that she would need to suspend disbelief for the time being, at least until she had a better idea of how this world, and its magic, worked.

Anandra hummed quietly as she checked the steak every now and again, and once it looked and smelled just right to Iris, Anandra took it off the grate and put everything besides it back in her bag, after her second time blowing on the flames seemed to extinguish them. Next she removed a large plate from her bag, and a fork and knife, and two glasses and a pitcher. That was almost the end of the rope for Iris's planned suspension of disbelief, because the pitcher held some pale-pink liquid, which should have spilled from its wide-open top as they trekked across the land and as Anandra went up against the two dangerous creatures. She might have been a skilled fighter, but this just didn't seem possible.

"How the hell did you manage not to spill that?" Iris blurted out.

"Magic, silly girl. Some of the items in this bag aren't even in it until I reach in there. The bag reads the owner's mind and provides what they want if it's capable of providing it. It's enchanted," she said as she poured the liquid from the pitcher into both glasses.

"Of course it's enchanted! I kind of could figure that out on my own." Iris might have thought not to blurt this out, too, but unlike her usual cautious self, she hadn't felt the need to hold her tongue. What kind of strange effect did this woman have on her? Normally, she wouldn't have even *thought* something like that to herself. She was barely capable of being mean on her worst days, and even then, her attempts at anger were pitiful.

"I'm sorry, was that rude of me?" A tone to Anandra's voice said she was teasing Iris, and Iris found herself smiling again as Anandra's mouth turned into a wide, lopsided smirk.

"No, it was rude of me, actually. I'm the one who should be sorry." Iris averted her eyes, her shyness flowing back over her like a heavy, suffocating blanket.

"All you should be sorry for is not eating your steak. We still have a good way to go before we reach my friends, and I'd like to get there before it's fully dark."

"I'll get started then," and Iris sliced off a bite and began to eat. The steak was perfectly cooked, and the drink turned out to taste somewhat like hibiscus tea. It was very refreshing after their long walk, and Iris finished her first glass and then asked for seconds. She managed to make it through two-thirds of her steak before she told Anandra she couldn't possibly eat another bite.

"I think you possibly could, and what's more, you don't have a choice. The magic won't work unless you eat the entire thing."

"Really? If you insist, then—"

"I do." Anandra leveled a glare in Iris's direction, and so Iris dug in once more, enjoying the rest of the steak less and less with each overly filling bite. She was so full she barely managed to choke down the last few morsels. No wonder her mom always cut their steaks into three pieces. Her dad Jerry always got the largest one, as he was the biggest of the three of them, but that was just because Iris and Jackie were rather petite.

She found herself missing Jackie and Jerry right then, more than she had in quite a while. She missed her professors, too, and even her roommates, even the one who always left empty pizza boxes and crusty glasses on their living room table. But most of all, of course, she missed Jane. What would she have made of this world? Would she have liked it here? Would she have liked Anandra?

Iris wasn't even sure if *she* liked Anandra. She knew next to nothing about her so far, just that she was great in bed and even better with a knife. And she could do magic. That was pretty much it, though, and besides, she'd only known her less than a day. Maybe over the time they were going to spend together on their trip to the castle, she'd have the chance to get to know her better. She surely wouldn't mind getting to know a few parts of her better…the very curvaceous parts of her, as well as the one that was very good at getting wet.

Anandra went back to her earlier quiet when they resumed their journey. She continued her silence for what seemed like forever, and Iris decided against trying to get her to talk. Her many hours spent around men in her own world had taught her that some people liked to converse even less than she did. She'd only really been comfortable talking around her parents and Jane, so her chattiness with Anandra surprised her. Maybe she liked her after all. Or maybe she just wanted to know more about this world, with its singing alligators and magic and women with starry expanses of skin.

It began to grow darker after what Iris would've guessed was four or five more hours of walking. They'd been passing along a wide dirt path for most of that time and hadn't come across a single person—or being—the entire time they were on it. As night began to fall, Anandra's stars began to glow, but not as brightly as they had the previous night.

"Do you have control over how much your stars glow?"

"Yes." A one-word answer; apparently talky-time was far over. Then, as a small grove of fruit-bearing trees appeared in the dusky distance, Anandra spoke again. "We're here."

"Here" turned out to be a mid-sized wooden cabin, with a small, snow-white dog sleeping on its porch. But when they came closer, the dog leapt up, began to growl, and quickly grew to twice its original size. "It's okay. Phen, Zeres, it's me!" Anandra whistled three notes on a rising scale, and the dog shrank again and settled back onto the porch, starting to snore as they approached. "He's not real, you know," Anandra told Iris as they reached the porch's two steps. "He's just an early warning system, for anyone who's approaching and may prove to be a threat."

The cabin's front door creaked open, and a mid-sized man with long, frizzy, umber hair stood in the opening. His wide smile showed that he had over-developed canines, lending him a vampire-like quality. Iris had always thought vampires were cool, although she'd never really wanted to meet one. Did this guy expect blood in trade for them spending the night under his roof?

"Is he a vampire?" Iris whispered to Anandra.

"I don't know what this 'vampire' thing is you speak of," the man said, proving that he at least had a vampire's hearing. "Zeres and I are both from a smaller group related to Anandra's. A much smaller one." He looked sad as he said this, and Iris wanted him to smile again.

"It's very nice to meet you," she said as warmly as she could.

"And you as well," he answered, clasping her hand between his very warm palms. "Welcome, Anandra's friend. I hope we will have enough food for both of you. Forgive me, but we weren't expecting Anandra to bring company. She always travels alone." He squeezed her hand once, then let go.

"My name is Phen, and you will get the pleasure of meeting my partner Zeres as soon as you come in. So, please, come in!" He opened the door wide, and Iris entered first, Anandra close behind.

The cool night air was instantly replaced with a lovely, gentle warmth that seemed to come from a snapping and crackling blue fire in a round brick fire pit in the room's center. Around the pit were comfortable-looking tan-cushioned chairs, and a large chicken, or something that looked quite like one, was roasting on a spit over the flames. It smelled divine, and Iris said just that.

"That's all Zeres's doing," Phen told Iris, and then she took in the man standing by the pit, slowly rotating the bird. He looked similar to Phen, the same type of teeth showing when he grinned at her and Anandra, but his hair was much shorter and tamer, and was a slightly paler shade of brown.

Dinner consisted of the bird, called a postrade (of course, Iris couldn't help asking), a large salad, and some very good alcohol, quite similar to red wine but slightly smoother. Iris tried not to drink too much of it, because if she and Anandra were going to have some fun that night, she wanted to be completely present.

She was happy to learn that they'd be staying in a small, two-windowed room far off in back of the cabin. Once inside, Iris set her bag down by the door, and then Anandra spoke in a voice that told Iris exactly what she had in mind for the next part of the night. "You can make as much noise as you want in here," Anandra told her, dropping her bag in a chair next to the door and turning her intense eyes to Iris. "They won't hear a thing."

It sounded almost like a threat the way she said it, but it clearly was only the threat of some very hot sex. Iris found herself wishing then that they could try out something kinkier than last time. She knew enough about the implements for BDSM that she found herself easily picturing a paddle, and she gasped in shock as one suddenly hit the room's big, comforter-covered bed. Her mouth fell open slightly from the sight. "How the…what…"

"Ah, I see we've discovered the power the meat gave you! Apparently it worked."

"The ability to bring sex toys out of thin air?" Iris asked. "How useful can that be?"

"Oh, I think it's already proving to be very useful," Anandra said to her, in a voice that told Iris *exactly* how useful she thought it was. She picked up the paddle and gave the bed a hard whack with it. The bed shook for a moment, and Iris began to grow a little wet…no, she thought, more than a little.

"What do you call this implement?" Anandra asked her. "Is it for spanking, perhaps?"

"Yes, it is." Iris's answer came out breathily. Expectantly.

"Take off your clothes, then. I will be more than happy to use it that way."

Iris quickly stripped off the clothes Anandra had loaned her and waited for the next instructions. She only had to be patient briefly, because after skimming her body with an assessing and then pleased look, Anandra said, "Now get on the bed. Chest and knees down. Ass in the air."

Iris did as directed, climbing over the left edge of the bed and assuming the position Anandra had described. It wasn't one she was used to, and she wasn't used to being spanked, either. She'd read up on all kinds of BDSM facts her first spring at college, wanting to know what else sex had to offer. It wasn't that she didn't enjoy what she and Jane did—orgasms with a partner did, indeed, beat orgasms alone—but something was missing. When she'd read up on BDSM on her laptop, alone in her dorm room, she'd practically felt chills of excitement, but whenever Jane came over, she hid all hints that she'd been looking up something that hardcore. Jane wouldn't have been interested and might have even teased her about it. But it had affected Iris, the reading she'd done, and as Anandra approached her, standing by the side of the bed she now knelt on, she realized this was why.

Yes, it had been arousal, that tension she'd felt in her spine and limbs, more immense than usual, more immense than Jane was able to bring out of her with her mouth and hands alone. She and Jane had never done anything even the slightest bit edgy, sticking to hands, mouths, fingers, and the occasional dildo. And all that time, Iris realized now, as Anandra raised the paddle…all that time, this had been what was missing.

Anandra brought the paddle down, and Iris gasped at the pain. It stung, which she should have expected, but the sting came along with a delicious heat that spread straight from the ass-cheek that had been struck to her thighs and cunt. Wetness began to move across the very highest part of her thighs, and she knew she was in for a good time.

The second time the paddle came down it hurt far worse than the first, and it seemed that Anandra wasn't going to take it easy on her, even though Iris assumed she knew exactly how new to this she was. It was, of course, brand new, leaving her unaware of what parts of kink would do it for her and which wouldn't. This part *did* do it for her, though, as she clenched all over, even tightening inside, between her legs, her hands beginning to grip the soft comforter beneath her.

Each time the paddle came down, she became more desperate for release, because her arousal grew a tiny—and then not-so-tiny—amount with each smack across her ass. "Please," she begged, softly, as Anandra raised her arm yet again.

"'Please' what? Don't tell me you've had enough, my pet."

"No, no, it's just…may I come?"

"Only if you can manage to get off while I continue to work your ass with this paddle. I want the pain of it to mingle with the delectable, lovely fall into coming that I'm assuming you'll get to quickly. I'll give you ten more smacks, and if you haven't come by then, you'll just have to go to sleep with an aching ass and an aching cunt that hasn't had its proper seeing-to."

"I'll try. Just…pause between each time?"

"You think you can make *another* request? Oh no, I'm not going to take my time, not at all." And with those words, she brought the paddle down twice, hard and heavy. Iris began to breathe more quickly, partially from the paddle and partially because she'd started to rub her clit with her first two fingers. From the corner of her eye, she saw Anandra switch the hand the paddle was in, and then she felt Anandra's fingers on her wetness, and two of them slipped inside her with ease. Anandra began to fuck her with those fingers, and Iris almost wanted to thank her for the help, because she felt she had almost no hope of getting off before the other eight smacks of the paddle occurred.

There was number three…then number four…and with each strike landing squarely on her ass, Iris sped up her fingers bit by bit, until she was sure they were a blur. Anandra continued to finger-fuck her slowly, only speeding up as the paddle hit for the seventh time. Number eight came a while after, thankfully, and Iris was shocked, because she was getting close. *So* close, and there was number nine, and then, with a blur of speed, Anandra began to fuck her much harder, and the tenth smack came raining down, and Iris came with a loud cry. Her body was shaking, now, from the orgasm and from the final smack of the paddle, and she continued to cry out and then collapsed on the bed as the coming ceased. She smiled, rolled over, and stared up into Anandra's eyes. "Your turn?"

Anandra ordered Iris to give her two orgasms, and Iris provided them happily, still blissed out from her spanking and how powerfully she'd gotten off. This woman really could screw, she thought, grinning as she climbed into bed beside her. Then her bedmate proved that she was quite competent at spooning, too, pressing her sexy front against Iris's still-sensitive backside and causing Iris to say, "Ow!"

"Oh, dear, you're sore, aren't you? Did I do it too hard?" She sounded genuinely concerned, which Iris found touching, and she quickly reassured her that she was more than happy with the service her ass and crotch had received.

"Good, because now the complaint tree is closed for the night. Time to sleep, as we still have many miles to go. Try to get enough rest, because I have a feeling you'll want to be as alert as possible tomorrow morning."

"Will do," Iris answered.

But she wasn't planning to sleep yet, and once Anandra's breathing had evened out, she quietly got out of bed and removed her diary from her bag, along with one of her pens. It was convenient that she still had them, convenient and annoying, because she'd promised her therapist that while she was in Amsterdam, she'd do an exercise, an "assignment." Uma had told her to write Jane a letter every night, telling her why she no longer needed her in her life.

Here goes, Iris thought, and she set pen to paper.

Dear Jane,
I miss you. I can't help it, I do! I still want you back, and I can't help it, but I still feel like I need you, no matter what Uma says. She may be a smart

therapist, but she clearly doesn't understand that I still love you an incredible amount.

But I should probably tell you—just like you did—I've met someone. She's gorgeous and amazing in bed...better than you, I could say. She definitely doesn't rank higher than you do in my heart, though. I barely know her, after all. But Anandra (that's her name) is interesting so far, and she's shown me many new things.

Including what was missing from our sex life. If I ever get back together with you again, I want to try these things with you. Kink, that's what I'm talking about...BDSM. Topping, bottoming, pain and pleasure co-mingled. She's pulled my hair, forced my mouth against her breast, and spanked me, and I've loved it all. I hope you will understand, if we ever sleep together again. I hope you will want to do these things to me, because I've come to know that they're a part of my makeup, just like loving you is.

(Yes, Uma. I know I'm supposed to tell Jane why I don't need her. But I can't. Not yet.)

I love you, Jane. Still do, with everything I have to give. Please take me back. Please.

Love,
Iris

After signing the never-to-be-sent letter, she put her diary and the pen away and got into bed, tossing and turning for an hour or so and then drifting into a sleep full of dreams of Jane and of signs that they would never get back together, signs she wasn't ready to recognize quite yet.

CHAPTER FOUR

Iris was happy to wake up later the second morning than she had on the first. Anandra was sitting in the chair by the door, sharpening her knife on a long, rounded silver rod. "Ah, rise and shine, Princess. You seemed uneasy during the night, so I decided to let you get an extra bit of sleep."

"Thank you, Anandra. I really needed it, I think. Yesterday was exhausting, but then I couldn't get to sleep." She yawned and rose from the bed.

Anandra reached into her bag and tossed something at Iris. It was a pair of panties, sexy lace ones with crisscrossed ribbons at the sides that connected their front and back. "My sack decided to be generous with what I'm giving you to wear under your clothes. I do not know this fabric that they are made from, but this sack is always imaginative when it comes to certain needs."

Iris assumed she knew what those "certain needs" were and found herself pouting a little at the thought of other women fulfilling those needs. But she still wanted Jane, and she barely knew Anandra, and she would only know her for a few more days before she was able to return home. "Do I get breakfast before we leave?"

"Yes, and Zeres makes a fine egg-pocket. He fills it with

cheese from their animals, and we will probably have some finely made cheefen. He's always been a better chef than I and refuses to tell me any of his tricks, the scuene."

"Scuene?" Iris started to put on her clothes from the previous day and get ready to leave the cabin.

"They are short, pink animals. Portly, full of fine milk and fine meat, but rather ornery. Like you are when going too long without cheefen, I would assume. Or whatever it was you called your world's version. Come, let us eat our breakfast, and then we'll be off."

The egg-pocket, which was basically an omelet, was filled with vegetables and rich, creamy white cheese, and Iris couldn't manage to compliment Zeres enough on how good it was.

"Ah, you say so, do you?" he said, smiling somewhat bashfully. As they ate breakfast, he told Iris that Anandra had brought him and Phen together, about fifteen sun-cycles after the Great War.

Anandra spat right after he mentioned the war. "We will not speak of that on this lovely day."

"And *you*, my dear woman, will not spit on my floor. You are not a scuene, after all. I would never allow them into my kitchen, the foul creatures."

"I apologize, my friend. I meant no harm. Except to the one who cost my parents their... As I said, we will not speak of it." She rose from the table and wiped her mouth with the back of her hand. "We will be off now. Thank you for your fine food and kindness in letting us stay here."

"You are more than welcome," Phen replied, and he enveloped her in a tight hug. "You be careful," he said softly, and Zeres nodded. "I don't want one of my best friends getting into any trouble on her journey."

"I will be, I promise. Iris?"

"Yes, I'm ready." Iris cleaned her mouth on the napkin by her plate and got up. After saying her own brief good-byes, she exited the cabin behind Anandra. Once she was back under the morning's slightly warm sunlight, she tried her best to steel herself for whatever might come next on their travels.

As they walked, she asked Anandra about the plants they passed by and the land they passed over, but after a while she ran out of questions and just enjoyed watching Anandra's backside swish back and forth subtly as she walked. It would be worth watching for a great number of hours, she decided just as they reached a rise in the road.

Now the sun was much higher in the sky than when they'd left that morning. Iris had been handling the stretches of silence as best she could. What was it about this woman that drew her out into the open like this, making her want to chatter away like a squirrel? She'd asked Anandra more questions during these two hours of walking than she ever could have come up with when at home or at the college. More than she even would have asked Jane. But Jane was the one who usually carried the conversation whenever they talked, and Iris hadn't minded that. She decided now that she *did* mind not knowing more about Anandra, and she got ready to ask her something, when suddenly, Anandra spoke.

"That's the guard of the town we must enter down there. Once we are in the town, please don't agree to barter or trade, because that could end disastrously. You do not know who is to be trusted and who is not. And I will need to be the one doing the speaking with the man down there. Not you."

"Well, if you insist."

Anandra chuckled softly. "I do, my dear, I do."

The man at the bottom of the rise was sitting on a small

wooden crate, peeling something that looked like an apple and humming to himself with his eyes shut. He appeared to be missing a leg, a beautifully carved wooden one in its place.

"How do you, beggar?"

"Quite well, dearie, quite well. What can I do for you?" He opened his eyes now, and they seemed filled to the brim with knowledge, lighting up as their intelligent gaze traveled from Anandra to Iris.

"I would like to enter Rivest. What do I need to give you in order to do so? I hear the usual price is answering a riddle."

"It's a nice day, innit? A nice day for a story. I insist I tell you one, and then we may talk about my fee for entry to Rivest." The beggar shifted slightly in his seat and shut his eyes. "Once, once there was a good Queen who ruled our land with kindness and love at her husband King Eurus's side. King Eurus wanted an heir, though, and for ten years Queen Selehn tried to bring him one, to no avail. Finally, in her thirtieth year, she became pregnant. He was saddened, when, upon entering the birthing chamber, there lay a baby girl in his wife's arms. But what could the King do?

"After a while, he began to mistreat the good Queen, calling her names…ugly, worthless, and even unfit as a wife. And then…then a thief came to the castle. A female thief, mind you. She stole the King's gold and stole his wife's heart, and the two women took off into the wilderness after falling madly, madly in love.

"The King, though, he remarried, and the next Queen, Tressa, she definitely was *not* good. She ruled the land with an iron fist and an iron heart, raising taxes and enslaving those unable to pay, forcing the men and women to erect for her a magnificent statue with a labyrinth within it, one no mortal or being of magic could ever solve.

"As her power grew, she brought an evil dealer of magic to the castle and began to create evil things, things as evil as her. They were formed in clay and then became monsters, and they threatened to take over the—"

"I do not care to hear any more." Anandra sounded as furious as she'd sounded when Zeres mentioned the war, if not a good bit more so.

"Oh, but I think your lady-friend is intrigued, is she not?" He nodded at Iris, smiled, and then continued telling the tale. "The evil Queen Tressa raised her monsters, and then she set out to take over the land. But she was unaware that someone else had also been given much magic, possibly more than her: the good Queen Selehn, of course. And so the two women met, and fought, and then…"

"And then *what*?" Iris was on the edge of her seat, or would have been if she'd been sitting down.

"And then, dearie, they disappeared, and so did the evil monsters, and were never heard of again."

"Are you done, then, beggar?" Anandra practically growled out the words, and it was beyond obvious that she was not happy. "Now the riddle?"

"Yes, dearie, now the riddle. Why do the stars shine brightly at night?"

Anandra huffed out a sigh. "Oh, really? You're going to go with one even a babe could solve? Well, if you *must*. The stars shine brightly at night because our first Queen gave the sky her jewels."

"I see she gave you some too, missy." And under his breath he added, "Grouchy missy, that is."

"I heard that, beggar! But now you must allow us into Rivest. So, if you don't mind—"

"I don't, not at all." The beggar lifted up his wooden leg,

and the designs carved into it began to move and twist around on it. He tapped its foot on the ground three times, and the land behind him began to shimmer, somewhat like a mirage, and an image began to appear.

After a few minutes, an entire city had appeared before them, and many buildings, made of rose-colored bricks and of varying heights, spread out across Iris's entire view. She could hear the bustle and chatter of what sounded like many people, and as she and Anandra began walking down the wide street that served as the entry to the village, she realized that they were passing through a marketplace. A gigantic one! Stalls lined each side of the road, which was wide enough for the many small carts pulled by various races and creatures, all passing them every few moments as they continued to walk. There were blue goat-like creatures, with curving horns and kind faces; foot-high people with their hair in black braids; and even one young man who seemed to be Anandra's race, who bowed to her, and to whom she bowed back.

The stalls were just as varied as the people and creatures, selling different-sized glass jars full of powders and liquids, scrolls, colorful piles of what looked like spices and herbs, meat still in the shape of the animal—or person!—it had come from, and then, after five minutes or so of walking, they reached a building with a dark awning, and a sign, covered in some sort of foreign text, hung above its closed, shuttered windows.

"Wait outside," Anandra told her. "*Right* outside. And don't go anywhere," she added, as though Iris didn't get what her first two sentences meant.

"Sure thing, boss!" Iris said with a jaunty salute and a sarcastic tone.

"I am not your boss, I am your friend," Anandra said, and

with those surprising words, she entered the building, opening its windowless door and shutting it behind her.

"Well, then," Iris announced to herself. "What to do now? Should I go somewhere?"

"You can go anywhere you like, young lady," came a voice to her left.

That was what she got for talking to herself—an answer. The voice came from a woman wearing a crimson cloak and a tight satin dress. She also looked almost as young as Iris was, her beautiful face empty of wrinkles and her blond hair luscious and shiny. "Young lady? But you must be only…I probably shouldn't be talking to you." Iris looked at the ground and began to rub the tip of her boot in the tan dirt.

"Maybe. But perhaps I can help you, too." The woman smiled at her, a feline smile, sexy but also potentially untrustworthy. Still, Iris decided she could use all the help she could get in this strange place.

"How can you help me?" she asked the woman, almost afraid of what the answer might be.

But then she heard the sound of the store's door opening, and Anandra came out, and by the time she reached Iris's side, the woman was gone.

"Were you talking to someone?" Anandra sounded even grouchier than she had when she'd left Iris outside, and Iris guessed it was because she'd noticed her talking to the young woman.

"You sound grumpy," Iris replied, trying to avoid answering and showing her what a bad liar she was in the process.

"Oh, I got robbed in the store."

"Robbed?" Iris's eyes went wide.

"Yes. The magic dealer in the store practically made me sell my first-born in order to get these stones," she said, holding up a small bag with a ribbon tied around its top. "I had to pay her at least a month's earnings from my deliveries and rescues."

So that was what she did for a living. "Can't you just make money with your magic?"

"Yes, but no one will accept it. They can all smell the magic on it, and all beings and people in our world find both its existence and its smell distasteful. Smells like a ripe scuene pen in mid-August."

"What next? Where to, I mean?"

"To a meal. I will try and find us a proper place, one with proper food and proper drink. Follow me." Anandra gave her a grin, looking as though she was glad to be there with Iris, or at least glad to be there.

Iris took in as much of the city as she could while they passed through it. She figured they probably wouldn't be staying long, so she might as well take in its many curiosities and wonders while she still had the chance. It didn't seem likely that she'd ever be able to return, and they might not even pass through another town on their journey to the Queen's castle.

The city was full of interesting people, awesome beings, and far beyond a few other sights of great interest to Iris's excited eyes and mind. She wanted to ask Anandra questions about everything, but she managed to limit herself to just five or six of them as they walked down the street, past more stalls and stores and what looked like restaurants and places to stay or live.

Anandra seemed more than happy to answer her questions. She sounded like she was in a jolly mood now, and Iris remembered as she walked that Anandra had called her a "friend." *Her* friend. Iris was more than okay with that title. She'd come to like Anandra, including when she was outside of the bedroom and with her clothes on. Iris would be slightly sad when their time to part came at the end of this journey.

She was thinking that slightly sad thought when Anandra stopped in front of a door with a sign hanging above it, showing a man and woman drinking out of what looked like beer mugs, and with more unfamiliar text above the art, although this sign had a different language than the last one she'd looked at.

"Ready to eat?" Anandra started to open the door.

But then something made Iris look over her shoulder, and what she saw beyond it caused her to gasp and grab at the door's handle for support. Less than five yards away stood a woman, facing away from Iris and heading farther away from her with a slow, smooth gait. She had long, curly white hair, and a loose, sky-blue summer dress hung down to her sneakered feet.

"No. No, it couldn't be." Iris blinked twice. *No, it couldn't!*

But it was. It was her grandmother, Sallie, who'd raised her to the age of ten. And then she'd disappeared, and Iris hadn't seen her since, despite looking for her everywhere and even going so far as to hire a private detective when she was twenty. Sallie had clearly loved her, and Iris had loved Sallie back. Of course, she still did. Seeing Sallie for the first time in over a decade, standing in the middle of Rivest in this magical, bizarre world, was almost too much for Iris.

But it wasn't enough to stop her from taking off running in her grandmother's direction. Iris reached her and grabbed at her arm, but it was as though she was made out of smoke, or mist, because Iris's hand went right through her. Instead of being able to take hold of her grandmother's arm, she felt her own arm being grabbed, and she stumbled as Anandra held her in place.

Iris whipped around. "Why did you stop me?"

"It's not safe for you to run off like that." Anandra sounded truly concerned, and Iris slowly let go of her tension, just like Uma had taught her to.

"It's just that...I think...never mind." For some reason, Iris decided not to tell her. She'd seem crazy, for one thing, because her grandmother was no longer there, almost as if she hadn't even been there in the first place. And maybe she hadn't.

"Whatever it is you think," Anandra said, "*I* think we should go in and get our lunch. And possibly something with a bite to it to drink. You need to cool off, and it's not just the hot sun that you need to get away from. Whatever you were running at, or for, it's not there, and even if I can't find out what it was, I still think it's in your best interests to stay focused on our travels and letting me keep you safe."

"Sure, you're probably right." Iris held in a sigh, just like she always did around Jane, who didn't like her acting dejected, or "dramatic," as Jane had usually called her when she'd sighed out loud.

"I am most definitely right!" The lovely grin was back on Anandra's face, and she and Iris went back to the restaurant's front door.

Just as Anandra entered, Iris heard a voice say, "I'll try again soon, sweetie." It was her grandmother Sallie's voice, no doubt about it. Iris was glad that Anandra was facing away from her when she heard Sallie's voice, because she knew the shock was shaping her face into an expression that would have led Anandra to give her the third degree. Possibly even the fourth.

They continued into a cool room full of people enjoying large plates of food and equally large glasses of alcohol. Most of the men were big and burly and hairy, and most of the women wore low-cut dresses and short skirts and too much makeup. Even the waitresses and bartender fit those profiles, the waitresses wearing short leather skirts and belly-baring, tight white tanks, and the bartender had copious amounts of dark hair peeking over the top of his shirt, more than enough of it to make up for his balding head.

"Sit anywhere you like," a long-haired, curvaceous waitress told them.

"Sit by me!" an inebriated voice called out. It belonged to a man the size of an ox, or at least three times the size of Iris. *Great*, she thought, *loads of drunk men whom I'll have to share the ogling privileges with.* Clearly, she and Anandra were going to be ogled as well, which Iris was far from happy about.

"Let's eat and get out," she said quietly near Anandra's ear.

"You have nothing to worry about," Anandra assured her. She sat at a table close to the door, in a chair that faced the bar and the bartender and had its back to the wall. Her choice of seat seemed to imply she didn't mean her words to Iris. But maybe she always sat in a spot where she could see the whole room; maybe she always sat in a spot where her back was to the wall; maybe she was just paranoid.

Iris couldn't blame her in a place like this, though. Certainly not! She did her best to keep from making eye contact with any of the men staring at her and Anandra, instead looking down at the menu the sexy and scantily clad brunette had brought them. She wasn't nearly as hot as Anandra, but there was no harm in looking in a place like this. Iris knew—or at least hoped—that she'd be able to check her out more subtly and less creepily than the manly men scattered throughout the place.

She couldn't read the menu, though, and suggested Anandra order for them. "Two bowls of the fish stew, with extra bread. And your finest alcoholic cider."

"We have erhna cider and that's it. Is that what you want?" The waitress, whom Iris had first thought attractive, now had a very *un*attractive sneer on her face. Yep, Anandra was definitely better looking. Maybe she and Anandra, with their relatively untrashy outfits, didn't fit in. From the way the heavyset man at the next table over was looking at them, though, they fit in well enough for the male customers. As the waitress walked away, Iris watched him warily out of the corner of her eye as he stared holes through her shirt.

"Maybe we should eat quickly after all," Anandra said to her, also eyeing the creepy man. "I don't like the way he's looking at you, like you're a juicy steak he's about to throw on the fire."

The waitress brought their food, and Iris was surprised to find out that the fish stew was rather good—rich, salty, and full of flavor. She detected some herbs, even, surprising for a place like this. The cider, though, tasted like rubbing alcohol with a hint of fake apple flavoring, and she noticed that Anandra wasn't drinking hers very fast either, although that might have been to keep her wits about her. Either that, or she also found it to be disgusting. Iris hoped it was both.

They were almost finished with their stew when things took a turn for the worse. Iris tensed up when she noticed the man who'd been staring at her slowly rise from his chair and walk over to their table, scratching his crotch right before he reached them. How utterly…charming. He had a huge, flushed red nose, clearly a few too many cups into his drinking for the day, especially considering it was lunchtime and not even close to nightfall.

"Hullo, womens. How's about you let m' join ya?" He flashed his teeth at Iris, more of a look of hunger than a smile, as if he wanted to devour her like some sort of savage beast. Not that he was too far from being one.

"Stop staring at her," Anandra ordered, and she gave him a very good glare. "Stop staring at her and leave us."

"Oh, the little, little lady wants me to leave, b'fore I've made friends with *her* friend. Not friend-*hic!*-ly at all, noshir." He placed his left hand on the table and started to reach toward Iris's shoulder with the other. But before he could find his way there, and before Iris could even blink, Anandra jumped up from the table and grabbed that hand, twisting it behind his back and pulling his arm in what looked to be an incredibly painful and unnatural direction. She kicked the back of one of his knees and he fell onto one lower leg, half-kneeling, and then she took out his other leg in the same manner, a loud, pain-filled grunt coming from him as each knee hit the floor.

"You will not touch her. She is with me. She is *mine*." She pulled his arm up a little farther and he cried out in pain.

Iris might have been impressed with Anandra's moves—very, very impressed—but she wasn't sure she was ready for Anandra to be calling her "mine." She was sure of one thing, though, and she became even more sure of it as their waitress approached the table, still sneering, but with a subtle touch of surprise added to the sneer. "You should leave. But first, pay. Or I'll sic the rest of them on ya."

"We will leave happily." Anandra slammed down some coins and headed toward the door. "And your cider is horrible," she added as she opened the door for Iris. "You should use it to give these scuene baths instead. It would be a much better use for it."

CHAPTER FIVE

Once they were outside again, Iris sighed deeply. "I couldn't be happier to be out of that hellish restaurant."

"Nor could I. I did *not* like how that ugly lump of man-scum was looking at you, and absolutely no way was I going to let him touch you. The nerve of that bastard! The nerve!" Anandra had slammed shut the building's front door—for good measure, apparently—but it seemed as if that hadn't been enough to dispel her anger at Iris's mistreatment.

"You know, Anandra," Iris said, patting her on the shoulder. "We're gone now, and we'll never see him again. Let's keep going and leave that prick as far behind as possible."

"Yes, we shall leave him far behind…and the cider, too, while we're at it."

Iris chuckled. The cider might have been disgusting, but the foul drunkard had still been far worse.

They continued down the street in the direction they'd been going, passing vendor after vendor, stand after stand, and also more people and animals and beings of many different types and sizes. Just before they reached what looked like the edge of the city, Iris smelled something delicious. "What's that tasty scent?" she asked Anandra, stopping for a few seconds. "It's so yummy it's almost making me drool."

"Those are fruitcakes, I believe. Eunberry ones, I'd wager." Anandra looked at her. "Would you like one?"

Before Iris could answer and tell her she shouldn't spend any more money on her, because she couldn't pay her back, Anandra strode over to the stand where a woman was selling the cakes and bought one after haggling over the price for a moment. "Here," she said to Iris, handing her a cloth-wrapped piece of cake. "You should eat it while it's warm. That way the fruit will still be nice and gooey."

Iris did as she was told, quickly taking a bite, and the jam-like filling oozed into her mouth, gooey, like Anandra had said, and very, very sweet. But not overly sweet—no, just perfect. "That...is so...good!" she mumbled around her mouthful of cake and jam.

"I'm glad you approve."

Iris looked down at the cake for a moment, and she noticed the cake was shaped like a heart.

As Iris ate the last of her fruitcake, they left the town, traveling down a dirt road that grew more and more narrow as they walked, and with each hour or so of walking, fewer and fewer people and beings crossed their path. Finally, it split into two narrow roads, and Anandra took the left one, and after that, just as the sun was almost down, they reached a large lake with tropical-colored water and large silver fish leaping out of it every few moments, shimmering in the sun's final rays of light.

"We will set up camp here," Anandra said, and she put down her bag. She reached in and drew a smaller bag from it, out of which she removed a small square item. She walked about thirty paces away from Iris, put the mysterious box down on the ground, and pressed its top. Then she ran back over to Iris and Iris heard a loud *pop!* from the direction of the box. Only seconds later, a tent practically exploded into view.

It was about the size of the cabin they'd stayed in the night before and was dark green and matte, with tassels and bells hanging from the corners facing toward them.

"Those bells only ring if danger is nearby," Anandra told Iris.

"Good to know. Can I check it out? The inside, I mean?"

"Of course. I think you'll be impressed. I thought you might like better accommodations than merely sleeping on the hard ground, so I purchased it from the same woman I got the stones from. I hope you like it."

"Thank you, Anandra. That was very thoughtful of you." Iris felt it was more than thoughtful, but she didn't want to press her luck or potentially scare Anandra with her level of appreciation. She'd never really enjoyed camping, even though she liked nature okay. It had rained every night when she was ten and she and her grandmother had gone camping, and then just a week later, her grandmother had disappeared. She thought back to the mirage she'd seen in Rivest, feeling an equal mixture of curiosity and sadness. Had that really been Sallie? Or had the midday sun just been playing a trick on her?

This camping trip, she told herself, would be much better, because she trusted that Anandra wouldn't disappear. No, this time, it would be she that disappeared, leaving Anandra's world behind. It really was a wondrous place, she thought as she walked over to the tent and opened its flap.

The tent's insides just added to the steadily growing awe she already felt, because it had to be the most pimp tent in the known universe. Or *universes*, if she happened to currently be in a different one than usual.

To begin with, the tent was much, much larger on the inside than it appeared from outside. A fire was roaring in a stone fireplace on its left wall, a four-poster bed with crimson silk sheets and almost too many plump, tasseled pillows sat against the back wall, and soft, sensual music was playing, coming from who knew where. Iris hadn't even known they had stereos in this world, but after looking around for one, she realized that magic yet again was causing the sexy tune to fill the tent with its mood-making intentions. Not that she needed help getting into the mood with Anandra. But sadly, that type of mood would have to remain unfulfilled, at least for the time being, because first, another need of hers required fulfillment: she was starving!

And Anandra had seemed to read her mind, because suddenly, a blanket appeared in the left side of the room near the fireplace, the room stretching to accommodate it. The blanket held various platters covered with fruit, cheese, and what looked like oysters. She also spied a bowl of small, square pieces of chocolate. Or something just like it, of course, because Iris suspected chocolate might not be available in this world. Just like DVDs, and coffee, and her favorite bookstore. She did miss her own world's version of coffee, and the bookstore, but when Anandra appeared at her side with a sly smile, Iris smiled right back and took the hand being offered, letting Anandra lead her over to the blanket, the fire, and the food.

"You should know that every item I have on this blanket is a known aphrodisiac of this world. The shelleuse, the ones in shells, are rumored to be especially potent."

"Oh, I don't think I need any help getting turned on by you," Iris exclaimed, but she still sat down and picked up a shelleuse, letting its salty, sweet contents slide into her mouth and down her throat.

"I don't know how aphrodisiacs work in your world, but they must be different there. Here, they give you more virility or, in our cases, more, and better, orgasms." Anandra winked at her and then picked up a small red berry, reaching forward and rubbing it across Iris's lips. She opened her mouth, and Anandra pushed the fruit inside, letting Iris's tongue taste her skin as well as the berry. She sucked on Anandra's finger for a moment as she tasted the fruit's sweet, yet still tart, flavor and then let Anandra feed her a square of chocolate.

It might have been the way Anandra was feeding her, or it might have been the food, but a flush came to her skin, followed by subtle tingles, and the twin sensations spread across her body and flowed down it until both of them reached her thighs and then her cunt. As delicious as the food was, she couldn't wait for "dessert."

She fed Anandra some of the food, too, but Iris ate lightly, not wanting to fill up before she had other parts of her body filled. They finished eating and shared a knowing look, and then Iris took Anandra's offered hand once more and let Anandra lead her to the bed.

The sheets were just as soft as they'd looked, the silk kissing Iris's skin as Anandra kissed her lips. "You taste even better than the food," Anandra said softly into her ear. Then she grabbed Iris's crotch, mashing her palm against it and bringing a high-pitched squeal of surprise from Iris's throat. "You didn't expect that, did you? I'd like to do a few more things you won't expect, just to get more delightful noises like that one out of you. Remember: I control you. I own you, until you leave this world. You are *mine*."

This time, Iris didn't mind being called hers...she didn't mind belonging to her. Because as Anandra stripped off her own clothes, and then Iris's, she found that right now, she wanted to belong to Anandra fully and completely. She wanted to let Anandra do as she wished to her flesh, to her body, to her cunt and tits and face. So when they were both undressed, and when Anandra brought back her hand and slapped Iris hard, she was shocked, but she was also pleased and aroused. Her cunt was wet, warm, and more than ready. And then, when Iris pictured ropes, and a strap-on attached to Anandra's hips, and when they appeared just as she wanted them to, she was more than ready to be tied up and entered.

"Your new skill doesn't leave anything to be desired, one might say," Anandra teased her, "but what is this thing I'm wearing? Is it meant to be inserted into you? Am I meant to fuck you with it? Is that what I'm supposed to do?"

"It's called a 'strap-on,' and that's a dildo attached to it, and yes, you put it inside a woman and you thrust it in and out of her."

"Like a man does?"

"Only way better."

"I'm game, then." Anandra grabbed Iris's thighs and shoved them apart, revealing her wet, hot cunt, showing exactly how ready she was to be fucked. "You certainly are ready... good girl! But not *that* good," she added with a wicked smirk. "Not good enough to avoid being tied up, although it seems you aren't even close to resisting such a thing."

"No, not at all," Iris said, her voice coming out breathy, both from the slap and from her more-than-obvious arousal and need. She wanted that dildo inside her, she wanted to be tied up, and she wanted all of it as soon as possible. She knew she wouldn't be able to come from the dildo alone, but she was so aroused by now it didn't really matter. She also knew that the food was only part of why she was so turned on, because her pleasure felt only slightly more intense than it had the two prior times they'd had sex. And it was bound to get hotter over time, wasn't it?

Anandra tied Iris's wrists to the top two bedposts, spreading her arms wide apart, making her helpless, which only caused her arousal to grow, and then tied each ankle to a bedpost as well. Then she began to tease Iris's hole with the dildo, seeming almost cruel as she denied her the penetration she so desperately desired. "Please, Anandra...please, put it in."

"You want me to slide this...dildo, was it?...inside you? You want me to thrust it in and out of you? Like a man? Only better? Much, much better? You're hungry for it, aren't you? You're hungry to be spread wide and shoved full of dildo, aren't you, sweetness?" And with that, she shoved the dildo inside Iris's cunt, every inch of it, and Iris made a long, loud, high-pitched cry of pleasure.

"Finally!" she gasped, as Anandra began to fuck her. And Anandra was like a natural, her hips undulating smoothly as the dildo slid in and out of Iris's opening, as it filled her up.

Anandra kept it deep inside her, only pulling it out a bit, and somehow, Iris had managed to create a dildo that actually pleasured her clit. But she couldn't possibly figure out how it could be happening, because she had limited experience with dildos and no idea how those experiences could have taught her exactly how to picture this Dyke's Ideal Dildo™, one that would be more than welcome in lesbian-friendly sex-toy stores. She'd have to take it home with her, that much was certain. However, there was also a small chance that *Anandra* was doing this, in which case she'd have to take *her* home, instead. And maybe that would be a good thing.

Wait, where had that thought come from? After all, Anandra wouldn't possibly want to go home with her, and why should she? And furthermore, why on Earth, and why on...whatever this planet happened to be called, would she want Anandra to come with her, for that matter? Iris quickly shoved that thought away and went back, relatively easily, to letting herself concentrate on the pleasure rippling out from the dildo.

Yes, it was rather easy to return to paying attention to the pleasure the dildo was providing. The impossible-to-ignore sensations from its length traveled from the opening of her cunt, where the dildo slipped in and out of her, all the way up to her clit, and then they all flowed back down in a quick, intense movement, followed by another trip up to her clit and then back down…and another…and Iris was almost there, almost there, and then—but before that next, important wave of pleasure could reach her clit for that final, necessary time, Anandra withdrew the dildo in another quick, intense movement, although this one was just intensely disappointing.

"Why?" Iris whined. "Why did you take it out? I was so close, so…fucking…close!"

"Because, Iris, I get to come first." She sounded like she meant her words one hundred percent, and Iris instantly knew she wouldn't change her mind. She watched Anandra take off the strap-on (not without a little trouble, Iris was pleased to see), placing it by Iris's side. So close, Iris thought. So close, and yet so far! But then those petulant thoughts turned to thoughts of how much she'd enjoyed eating Anandra out at other times, and as Anandra straddled her head and lowered her wet pussy onto Iris's lips, she began to salivate in hunger for the second time that night.

Iris didn't even have to lift her head. Anandra brought the party to her, instead, placing her clit right about a centimeter away from Iris's lips. She rose up the miniscule amount required and opened her mouth. She intended this time to get Anandra off until she couldn't think, until her legs turned limp and so did her arms, until all of her did so as well. She wanted Anandra to know she'd chosen the right woman to sleep with, because all that time she'd spent with Jane had made her feel like maybe those words would never be true about her. She needed to feel she could succeed at properly pleasuring a woman, and so far she was doing just fine, judging from the way Anandra was already riding her mouth and telling her how good she was.

Yes, apparently she *was* good, because soon enough, Anandra's first peak came, and then, after maybe a minute, she had another. This time, she had Iris stop at the lucky number of orgasm number three, and then Iris got three of her own, Anandra working away at her clit with her fingers while she growled dirty things into her ear, things like what a slut Iris was, and how she was pretty sure she could even get into her ass without a fight. Iris was surprised at how aroused those words made her. Wait, she was into anal now, too? She was shocked at how her world had expanded in these last few days. First Amsterdam, then another universe, and now BDSM. Was anal next on the checklist?

But it wasn't to happen tonight, as Anandra got her off for the third time and then stopped, after having Iris clean off the hand she'd used with her tongue. She untied Iris and they climbed under the covers.

"What a dirty, dirty girl you are. I've never had this much fun with a partner, never!" Anandra quickly looked away after she said this, looking almost regretful.

Iris felt some regret herself. Maybe it'd have been better if they'd kept business and pleasure separate. After all, they'd each be going their own way in only a few days, and she couldn't let herself get the least bit attached to this admittedly beautiful and charming woman.

Anandra looked back at her then, and Iris was struck again by her beauty. No one she'd seen on Earth in all her years could have rivaled this woman, but Anandra was almost cheating, what with the glowing cosmos scattered across her perfect, supple flesh.

"Does your star-covered skin serve a purpose?" Iris asked.

She instantly realized how rude her question was when Anandra replied, "Does *yours*?" But then she smiled at Iris and took her hand. "I have heard it was to help our ancestors find their way through the darkness and to connect them to all the power of the universe. Or something like that. But for me, it's just a way that I stand out from others who aren't like me. I suppose I'm all right with looking this way, for it's how I've always looked, but it reminds me too much of...of..."

And then a single, glowing tear dropped from Anandra's eye all the way down to where she held Iris's hand in hers. She cleared her throat and began to roll over. "I think we should go to sleep now. Got to get started early tomorrow morning, you know." She sounded gruff as she spoke, but Iris could still hear the anguish that had caused the tear. It seemed like there was some loss in Anandra's past, something perhaps similar to the loss Iris had experienced. She guessed it might have something to do with the war that Anandra never wanted to talk about, but instead of prying and trying to get to the bottom of it, Iris spooned her and shut her eyes. Anandra tensed at first, but then she relaxed moments later, and soon she was asleep.

It might be time to write another letter, Iris thought as she waited for her own sleep to come, and when it refused to, she decided she had no choice but to comply with her annoying therapist's advice. She climbed out of bed and got her bag, removing her notebook and pen and sitting crossed-legged on the rug. Where to begin, where to begin...

Hello again, Jane. It almost seems like I've lived a lifetime since I wrote the first letter in this notebook. It feels like something has changed since last night, and I can't quite put my finger on what it might be. Nothing has changed about how I feel about you, though. I still love you, very much, and I still think I'll try, one last time, when I get home…try one last time to lure you away from that bastard and back into my arms.

But maybe…maybe we weren't as perfect of a fit as I thought, at least sexually. Something to work on, I suppose, if I can ever get you back with me and back into bed with me once more. I don't know…it's been amazing, absolutely amazing! With Anandra, I mean. All this BDSM that she and I have been doing has shown me why I couldn't even come close to getting entirely into it with you, no matter how hard I tried. It must be why I get off so much faster with her, cutting my time to orgasm in half, and then some! I don't think you're to blame, because Anandra can't be all that much older than you. Although maybe beings, people or whatnot, age differently in this world and…

Iris paused. She couldn't let her therapist see that part, no way. She'd think Iris was crazy. So she scratched out those words and wrote a new sentence in their place.

Who knows, though? She may be more experienced than you, or she may just be able to read me better. Maybe I'll even be better in bed by the time I return home. Maybe I'll be able to teach you a few moves.

Iris wanted to cross that part out, too, but instead she just laid down the pen and then put it and the notebook back in her bag. She got into bed again and let the sound of the crackling fire and its warmth help her finally drift off.

It couldn't have been that much later when Iris woke with a start. It was only then that she remembered her bad dream from the first night. But maybe it hadn't been a dream. Because right now, her chest ached slightly, and she knew you couldn't feel things in dreams, and because the tightness in her limbs and throat as she noticed the same dark figure from two nights ago was all too real.

Then the figure began to glow, its darkness turning to light as it approached the bed. "It" became "she" then, because it was clearly a woman. Iris watched as the woman became more and more defined, until with a sharp gasp she realized it was Sallie, her grandmother, who now stood mere feet from her, glowing white and wearing the same clothing she'd worn in the market.

"Hello, pumpkin. Oh, how I've missed you!" Sallie looked like she meant her words completely, or possibly even somewhat more.

"Well, knock me over with a feather!" Iris exclaimed, feeling a little dizzy at this sudden turn of events. Oh, no, was she going to faint again?

"You look almost as pale as I do, Iris. Do you need some water?" A look of concern passed over Sallie's face, the face more like mist than skin. Iris feared she wouldn't be able to get the hug she desperately wanted from this woman whom she hadn't seen in far too many years.

"No, no, I think I'll be okay," she told her grandmother, taking a deep breath through her nose and slowly blowing it out through her lips. She shut her eyes for a moment, half-afraid Sallie would be gone when she reopened them.

She was still there, though. For a few more seconds, at

least, but then Iris heard sounds coming from her left, and she turned to see Anandra jolting into an upright position. "What is it? Is someone there, Iris?"

There had been, or at least there'd been somewhat of a "someone," but now as Iris looked, her grandmother was gone. "I will try again, I promise. I will try to come back," she heard in a warm, kind voice, a promise she hoped her grandmother would be able to keep.

"No," she lied, keeping her head facing away from Anandra. "No one's there. I think it was some wild animals making some noise outside that woke us up."

"I'll go and check, then. You can never be too careful. That's what my father taught me when he began training me." Anandra quickly put her clothes back on and went outside the tent, slipping almost soundlessly through its front flaps.

She returned just as Iris was starting to fall asleep. "Just a few fish and a pair of mating Rainbow Nightbirds. You may go back to sleep, all is well." She surprised Iris by pecking her on the cheek, and this time Iris was the first to sleep, Anandra's warmth beside her chasing away any worries about her grandmother's strange reappearance. It would all get worked out in time, she told herself, forgetting in her drowsy haze that Sallie had been the one who had first given her those particular words of advice.

Chapter Six

I n the morning, Anandra announced that Iris was required to give her an orgasm before they took off, and who was Iris to say otherwise? So she ate Anandra out with almost as much pleasure as it was clear she was giving her in return. Anandra got a second orgasm for free, although she still insisted she pay Iris back later. "Maybe we'll find somewhere we can stop today for lunch that will be convenient and secluded enough for me to bring you an orgasm in thanks. I am grateful, of course, for your own generosity."

"There's a saying in my world: it's always better to give than to receive."

"And you seem to have taken it to heart!" Anandra gifted her with a happy look, then leapt out of bed and proceeded to get dressed, although first, she gave today's panties to Iris, this time a pair of pink satin boy-shorts with cutouts on each side and a low-cut waist. "Thank you, bag," she said to her satchel, then placed her hand over her heart and bowed to it. "You are a most generous accessory, worth every coin to see her in those sexy under-things." She gave Iris a not-so-subtle look, and Iris wished then that they had enough time to get her off, too. But only for a moment, because Anandra rushed her into her clothes and out of the tent, barely stopping long enough to let her eat some toast and drink some cheefen.

"I know you'll be no fun to be around if you don't drink it," she told Iris, and Iris wasn't about to complain. She'd made it a habit to never look a gift latte in the mouth, and she was rather grateful that Anandra seemed to understand her intense need for caffeine in the morning. Especially when the sun had barely crested the nearby hills.

Iris almost didn't want to leave the fancy tent and the bed behind, though, even with the lift of the caffeinated cheefen. Or maybe it was magic, and not caffeine? That would make more sense. But it wasn't just the comfy bed and the early hour that made her want to stay, and it wasn't just Anandra's luscious lips, either. Anandra had warned her that she'd heard tell of vicious monsters living nearby, maybe a few hours from where they now were, and upon hearing that, Iris wanted nothing more than to stay behind, in bed, and have sex for the rest of the day. And to avoid those scary-sounding monsters while she was at it.

She had stopped herself from speaking up, though, because she had no other option. It wasn't as if she could travel back to Rivest and move in with some kindly shopkeeper, living out the rest of her days selling magical objects and avoiding the restaurant they'd eaten at the previous afternoon. That wasn't an option, and so, feeling scared but resolute, she grabbed her bag and followed Anandra out of the tent.

"We're just going to leave it there?" she asked, getting concerned when Anandra had started walking away from the tent.

"Yes, we are. It only expands, it doesn't contract. I got the cheaper model. We'll just have to find some other kind of lodging tonight."

"Tonight" was a long way off, though. They were getting off to their usual early start; too early for Iris, but she was almost getting used to it, and the sky on this particular morning was awash with reds, purples, and the lightest of pinks. It was beautiful, very much so, but Iris found her eyes traveling from the sky and back to the face of the woman who walked beside her. She was beautiful, too, also a sight to behold. Iris still hadn't gotten used to how striking her eyes were, her pale, long lashes accentuating their elegant, slight uptilt, and their rich, glowing jade green only one of the many parts of her face that would draw anyone's eye. She wouldn't have fit in were she to travel to Iris's world, to Earth, and that was just as well. Anandra belonged here, and Iris didn't. Besides, no matter what Anandra thought, she couldn't hold a candle to Anandra's exotic and awe-inspiring looks. She was more like a half-used birthday candle in comparison to Anandra's gold, crystal-draped chandelier.

"What might you be looking at, pretty lady?" Apparently Anandra had noticed her staring. *Great, just great.*

"Nothing, just thinking about last night." She felt a flush rising to her cheeks and hoped Anandra would think it came from her memories and not from what was really causing her to blush.

"And this morning, too, I hope?"

"Yep, that, too!" And now she was thinking about both of those times, and Anandra's naked body, and now the heat from her face traveled to other, lower parts of her body. Good. Her arousal might help to distract her from what lay in their path: the monsters Anandra had told her about.

But she was still unable to resist asking a question. "Are you sure those stones will work?"

"Ladies first," Anandra said, as they had just reached a narrow bridge that crossed part of the lake. "And yes, I was told that the stones could fell any creature they touched. We'll just have to hope my aim is as true as it usually is. Now, Iris, you will need to be careful as we cross this water. I have been warned about it as well. If you don't—Iris!"

It was too late for a warning. Iris had looked down into the water as she started along the bridge, to see if she could spot one of the beautiful fish she'd seen the previous night. And as she looked down, she began to see cracks in the water, like it was solid and about to shatter. And as she stared at the cracks, Anandra became farther and farther away from her with each passing second.

Anandra ran for her, reaching for her hand, while the cracks spread from the water to the bridge, and then even to the sky. Then there was a shattering sound, like a million glasses breaking all at once, and everything disappeared.

❖

"This hotel room is beautiful, Anandra."

"I'm happy you like it."

Anandra was standing by the window, lit up in a very attractive way. The stars on her skin were dimmer than they'd been when Iris had first met the beautiful street performer in the middle of the city. She'd been juggling bowling pins in a short, loose T-shirt and tight jeans, and Iris had checked her out as she walked by. Later, she'd seen the woman again, ordering coffee in a café near where Iris was staying, and Anandra had invited her to join her.

That had been a week ago. They'd quickly fallen into bed together, and Anandra had told her that, actually, she came from a very rich family, and would Iris like to stay at a room in one of their hotels instead of her own room? Iris had hesitated, but Anandra's lovemaking and her kindness had tempted her until she'd given in, and now they were in the penthouse suite of what had to be one of the nicest hotels in the city. It was also the fanciest hotel room Iris had ever been in, with a separate sitting area, a giant king-sized bed, and a Jacuzzi tub right next to the large floor-to-ceiling windows.

"You know, I've never had sex against those windows before. I think it would be a rush." Anandra ran the back of her hand down Iris's cheek and then grabbed her and held her tight against her own, suddenly naked body.

"What the...weren't you just wearing clothes? I could have sworn you were..." It was either the sudden nudity or the idea of having sex against the window that had given Iris a head rush, one so intense her knees shook a little when it flashed across her scalp.

"You aren't afraid of heights, are you?" Anandra pulled back from her, looking a little concerned.

"Well, yeah, I am, but...I'm up for it, I think."

"You *are*?" Anandra began to suck on Iris's ear while she waited for an answer.

That made the answer come swift and easy. "Yes, I am—very much."

Anandra spun her around, now facing toward the window, and walked her over to it. "Spread your legs and lean against it. I want my view to be as jaw-dropping as yours."

"Thanks," Iris said, but it came out high-pitched, the shock from her view shaking her resolve and taking away just a touch of her arousal. That touch of arousal came rushing back as Anandra fell to her knees, nipping at Iris's body here and there as she sank to the floor. She shoved Iris's legs a little farther away from the window, making her even more unsteady on her feet.

But all of her fear disappeared in the instant it took for

Anandra's mouth to find her pussy. Iris shut her eyes, her back arching slightly as Anandra reached an especially sensitive spot.

For some reason, though, she couldn't get completely lost in the sex. She was *mostly* lost in it, because Anandra was more than competent at getting her off, always going at just the right pace with her fingers or tongue. But she still couldn't get lost in it entirely, not like usual. Not at all like usual. Because now something was dawning on her, a strange thought that told her she wasn't supposed to be here. No, not here, even though she wanted to stay.

Anandra was doing such a good job, getting her so close, and the way her mouth felt on Iris's clit gave her sensations that were practically out of this world. But she wasn't supposed to be here, she knew this, and she believed it more and more as she also came to believe she was going to come, and soon.

No, she wasn't supposed to be here. She was supposed to be somewhere else, somewhere else where she actually belonged.

She hadn't become distracted enough to stop herself from coming, though, and as she shook against the window, and as her knees grew even weaker, she felt Anandra's nails sink slightly into the backs of her thighs, the pain only strengthening the power of her orgasm. Inevitably, the pleasure began to fade, and as it did, she remembered again: this wasn't where she was supposed to be, and this wasn't Anandra's world. She wasn't here; she couldn't be, not really, not when she belonged—

❖

The hotel room was gone, and Iris was staring at a river that was frozen in place, something stopping it from flowing as it should. All around it were wildflowers, and she could hear the buzz of bees and sweetness of birdsong coming from nearby.

"Where…where am I now?" Iris couldn't stop herself from speaking the words aloud, but someone was in front of her, so at least she wasn't talking to herself like a crazy person or anything.

But the sight in front of her was something a crazy person would imagine, or hallucinate, perhaps. In front of her was a woman with a strangely familiar face, with hair a brown close to Iris's own and a face Iris couldn't help trying to place. The woman sat in the middle of a giant lotus, floating at the edge of a river, her legs crossed and her hands resting gently in her lap.

When she answered Iris, she spoke in a voice that seemed familiar somehow, too, but Iris couldn't place it either. "You are in a second world you don't belong in, and it is time for you to return to the one you left."

"Which one?" Iris asked the woman. "Mine? Or Anandra's? And what's happening to me, anyway?"

"I wish you could stay," the woman said, which wasn't really an answer to her question. She looked at Iris with kind eyes and a sweet smile, then shut her eyes, rubbing at them with her hands as though something was irritating them. "You may not be able to trust everyone you come across in her world. I have a feeling you won't be able to. I don't know how long I can keep this portal open, though, so just know that I hope you succeed, and that you receive everything you've ever wished for, too. Not that you necessarily will, but I still hope for it."

"Who am I not supposed to trust, though? And who are you? Have we met somewhere before?"

"Yes," the woman answered, and now Iris could see that she was crying. "Yes, we have, Iris."

❖

Iris came to with lips on her mouth, and she knew instantly that this was not a kiss of passion, but a kiss of life. In the moment it took her to realize that the lips were Anandra's, she felt the sudden urge to cough, and she weakly shoved Anandra away, leaning to the left and coughing up some water. She wiped at her mouth with her hand, then slowly turned her face back to a very concerned-looking Anandra.

"What...what happened? I wasn't here, and you were there, and then you weren't and—"

Anandra placed a gentle hand on her shoulder. "Don't talk. Just try to get your breath back. You fell into the lake and began to sink, and I managed to loop my bag's handle around your wrist just in time. I must insist now that you disregard anything and everything you might have seen while you were lost to this world. The lake's water, I have heard, is enchanted, and everything you see and hear as you sink is only meant to keep you under its surface until it is too late. I thought it *was* too late for you, actually." Anandra got up off the ground and offered Iris a hand. "Did you see anything? I haven't heard of anyone ever surviving this lake's powers, and I do find myself wondering what the people who fall into it see. It must be appealing, whatever it is."

"The beginning of my vision was," Iris told her, and mustered up the strength to wink at her.

"Ah, I see, I see. You naughty girl. Was it me that distracted you so well that you forgot you were drowning?"

"Maybe." Iris took the offered hand and pushed up from the grass. She would have liked to lie there awhile longer, but she'd remembered what they'd soon be coming up against, and she wanted to get it over with. Almost drowning might have weakened her a bit, but the threat of monsters in their future, ones that Anandra had actually sounded afraid of, only added to the weakness she felt throughout her body. She began to wonder about the exact contents of the enchanted lake water. Could she get some sort of sickness from swallowing so much of it? Hopefully she wouldn't catch anything from it besides a few chills.

After walking in the sun for a few minutes, steadily heading away from the stupid, enchanted lake, the cold she'd been feeling had lessened a fair amount, and she told Anandra they could begin to move faster once more. Nearly drowning might have weakened her some, but she refused to let that stop her from keeping up their usual traveling pace. Nor would she let it stop her from getting the monster-filled part of their trip over and done with as quickly as they could. No, she would use her fear to power her on, she decided. Although anything that *Anandra* was afraid of was probably not good, and perhaps a little more threatening than what they'd come across so far.

But she didn't whine when Anandra suggested, after a few hours of walking, that they stop for lunch. Because while she did want to get past the monsters as soon as possible, and while she still was scared, she hadn't managed to lose her appetite.

"Our breakfast was so light that I think stopping early is a good idea."

"No complaints here," Iris said with some fake cheer. Well, it was partially real, but mostly her overly cheery tone was there to cover the tremor that was bound to come out at some point. They'd been getting closer and closer to the mysterious monsters with each step, Iris knew, and though Anandra might have been very brave, something about this particular threat had shaken her more than anything else had on their travels so far. And if someone wasn't afraid of a hungry, gigantic alligator, what *would* they be afraid of?

Iris dropped down into a cross-legged seated posture and placed her bag off to her side. They'd stopped by the road, about half a mile away from a forest that looked like a fire had traveled through it at some point. Its trees were burned black, but they still blocked whatever hid within them from their current vantage point. Iris hoped the forest didn't turn out to be as creepy as it looked from where she now sat.

"How much do you know about these monsters, anyway?" she asked Anandra as she tore off a piece of some proffered bread. She also took some sharp-smelling cheese that had been stored in a small wooden box, letting its equally sharp taste mingle with the full, yeasty goodness of the hard-crusted bread. She was momentarily distracted by the quality of the food while she waited for Anandra to answer.

"My village's Eye of the Future foretold various things about our travels. They advised me of what I might come across, including that on my third day away from home, I would encounter some very dangerous monsters. They didn't say anything else about them, hence my nerves being pulled a mite tighter than usual. I apologize that I don't have more information, but of course, our Eye is not all-seeing."

"The…Eye of the Future, or whatever, it didn't warn you about me?" Iris took another bite of bread and a swig of the juice that Anandra had pulled out of her bag when they'd sat down.

"No." Anandra turned her head away from Iris and took a large bite of bread. "No, it didn't," she mumbled through her full mouth.

Something told Iris she was lying, because although she'd known Anandra for only a few days, she still felt she'd picked up on a few of her cues. Hints of her thoughts and intents were usually obvious on her face, at least when she was talking to Iris. It was almost like she let her guard down around her, and Iris wasn't really sure what to make of that realization. Anandra didn't seem like the type to ever let her guard down, so Iris decided that, just like her guess that Anandra was lying, it couldn't possibly be true. Besides, she needed to trust Anandra, because she was the only thing that stood between her and these monsters in their path. She was possibly the only thing that stood between her surviving the monsters or becoming the monsters' supper.

"I would like to tell you a story, one that my mother told me when I was young. Are you game?" Anandra sliced off a sliver of cheese with her knife and ate it off the blade.

"Sure you aren't just procrastinating?"

It almost seemed that Anandra was blushing, but she wouldn't want it pointed out, so Iris just ignored the fact that she might have been embarrassed, instead settling into a more comfortable position and getting ready to hear whatever this story might be.

"Once, about fifty sun-cycles ago, our land's good Queen gave the King a child. But King Eurus was not happy to have a new member of his family, because the child was a girl. Over time, as sun-cycles passed and the Queen didn't give him a son, he grew cold toward her, becoming cruel and distant, more and more so with each passing month. In her child's fifth sun-cycle, a thief made her way into the castle and stole the King's golden lion."

"Golden lion?" Iris asked. "Was it made *out* of gold or just gold-colored?"

"It was made out of gold, but it was also alive. May I continue?"

"Sure, of course. Sorry."

"The golden lion was of more value to Eurus at this point than his wife, so when, strangely, the thief offered the lion in trade for his wife, the King said yes. But he didn't know that the thief had previously been in his employ, as one of the Queen's maids, and Queen Selehn and the maid had fallen in love. Before the King could change his mind, though, the Queen ran off and was never seen again. Until the Great War, that is. The war where I lost both my parents," she told Iris, and she stabbed her knife into the ground with a quick thrust as she burst into tears.

Iris couldn't have been more shocked if Anandra had exploded instead. "I'm so, so sorry. Can I do something?"

"A hug might be acceptable," Anandra said in a gruff voice, sounding almost angry. So Iris wrapped her arms around her, holding her to her breast for a few moments until Anandra pushed her away. She seemed to have stopped crying as quickly as she'd started, and she wiped her eyes on the backs of her hands, taking her knife and placing it back in its sheath. She dug a hole in the ground and buried the box that had held the cheese and the bag that the bread had come from, and put the juice bottle back in her bag. Each thing she did with a stoic, empty expression on her face, and Iris didn't know how to react, either to the sudden tears or the equally sudden cessation of them. "Are you all right, Anandra?"

"I am fine. Let's get this over with, so we may continue on our way with no further interruptions."

Iris rose from the ground and picked up her bag. Time for some monsters, she thought to herself, fighting to stop from freezing where she stood. She also had to struggle to keep herself from turning tail and running back the way they'd come. She had almost never been this scared, and of all the times for Anandra to fall apart! But she had to be honest: it had touched her deeply that Anandra had felt comfortable enough to share this part of her past. It had touched her very deeply indeed.

So, she decided, she would stay by Anandra's side for the time being, because although she'd seemed shaken a few moments ago—very shaken—Anandra seemed as if she was back to her usual stoic, brave self once more. Or at least as close as she was going to get in the time it would take them to reach the grove of burnt trees, the trees where the monsters they were to face just might be hiding.

CHAPTER SEVEN

They reached the trees in what seemed like no time at all. It might have taken them twenty minutes, but it felt like only one or two. My, how time flies when you're approaching something terrifying, Iris thought as Anandra placed a finger on her lips to hush her. Right, like she was going to start belting out show tunes to let whoever or whatever was hiding in these trees know she was there. Something was off-seeming about them, something creepy, almost like the trees were still alive, alive and watching them. But that was a silly thought, she chided herself. Very silly, although she'd seen plenty of things in this world weirder than sentient trees.

"Walk as softly as you can," Anandra said in an almost inaudible voice, close to Iris's ear. Normally, a whisper in her ear from a hot woman would have sent shivers down her back. This time, though, it wasn't the whisper that made her shiver—this time the shivers came from fear instead of arousal. Oh, how she wished it were the latter!

She'd already made up her mind to keep going, even with the threat of the terrifying monsters. So she followed Anandra into the trees as quietly as she could, hoping she wouldn't bungle their silent approach by stepping on a twig or sneezing. After about fifty as-silent-as-possible steps, she heard voices slightly in front of them. She and Anandra took about ten more steps in the voices' direction, and then they both hid behind the trees, at the edge of a clearing in the woods.

Within the clearing, three hideous creatures sat on large boulders, their voices almost more like hisses than normally spoken words. All of them were dark brown, and they looked like they'd been fashioned out of mud. Each had a mouth of oversized, long, sharp teeth, two completely black eyes, and two nostrils set in their face like you'd see in a skull. Iris had thought she was scared as they'd approached the woods, but the shakiness she'd felt throughout her body then had nothing, absolutely nothing, on how scared she was now. If she hadn't been smart enough to stop herself, she would have started running out of the woods as fast as her legs could carry her. But these beings also had large ears, the better to hear her with, most likely. Hopefully they didn't like how humans tasted, and hopefully, if they spotted her and Anandra before Anandra could take them down, Iris's death would be quick and merciful. But now the words the monsters spoke seemed to imply it would be anything but.

"We mussst do more damage than lassst time, Frud."

"I know, Gar. Ssshe told usss that ssshe wantsss thisss to go quicker. Kuk, you did not kill enough in the lassst village, either."

"Be quiet, Frud."

"But it isss true, you idiot. Kuk only killed twenty or twenty-five. *I* killed at leassst—"

"Be quiet!" The one he'd called Gar rose from his boulder, showing that he was much too tall for his own good. Or for Iris and Anandra's. "I heard sssomething in the treesss." Gar turned his head from left to right and made a loud sniffing sound. Oh, great, could he smell them?

"I knew it!" He started to walk right in the direction of

their hiding spot, and then Iris saw a stone go whizzing through the air and hit him squarely in the forehead, clearly Anandra's doing. Maybe they'd make it out alive after all!

Gar fell to the ground with a loud *thud*, but before Anandra could throw another stone, and quicker than Iris could blink, the other two monsters were upon them, grabbing the backs of their necks and lifting them off the ground. Iris saw Anandra sneak something into the back of her pants. She did this right before the two terrifying creatures started carrying them toward a cave. Either it had come out of nowhere, or she'd been so scared she hadn't noticed it. Whichever it happened to be didn't matter, because as they entered the cave, Iris saw a pile of bones to their left about a foot high. Apparently, the monsters were just as deadly as their words had implied. Apparently, this would be their final resting place. No one would even be able to send flowers if they were to die here. And no one Iris knew on Earth would even know what had happened to her.

The taller of the two remaining monsters bound their wrists behind their backs and then bound their hands together, taking Anandra's magic stones and placing them on the ground, out of reach. The shorter of the two monsters sat down in front of them, apparently to keep watch, or to start marinating them in sauce and spices, because the pile of bones probably hadn't been emptied of flesh on their own.

And here came her answer. "I am hungry," said the tall one, who she thought was named Frud. He started lumbering toward the cave's opening. "We will dine and then we will go to the nexssst village. I will go and make sssure Gar is dead."

"Yesss. We did not like him, though. It will be no losss if he isss."

"I agree," said Frud. "It is sssad that we cannot eat him."

"We have enough food now, though." A thin stream of

drool ran down Kuk's chin, and if these creatures were capable of smiling, that's what he was doing now, although he wasn't really doing it right, Iris decided. "Tonight we will feast as ssshe doesss."

Who was this "she" they were talking about? But before she could ask (yeah, like *that* was a good idea!) she felt a slight movement in each of Anandra's arms, almost like she was taking something out of her back pocket. Iris came close to asking her what she was doing, a clear sign that being scared out of her mind made her faculties perform at less than their usual speed and skill. The monster guarding them didn't seem to notice Anandra's stealthy movements, and instead of stopping Anandra from doing whatever she was trying to do, the imposing monster turned to face Iris and said, "I want to tell you a ssstory."

Iris figured her shock at Kuk's words was plain to see. These creatures hadn't seemed like they cared much for her and Anandra so far, so the fact that this creepy fellow wanted to play "story time" with her and Anandra would have seemed very unlikely if it hadn't just happened. "O…okay. Go ahead."

"I don't need your permisssion, woman. I only need you to lisssten." The creature glanced at the opening to the cave, then lowered its voice and turned back to Iris, looking straight at her and making her flinch from his powerful and hungry stare. "Onssse, our Queen made usss. Ssshe made usss from clay and from dark magic; ssshe made usss to help her rule thisss world. But the last Queen, Ssselehn, ssstopped her. Ssshe lowered our numbersss, killing usss off one by one. It hurt usss, each time a brother fell. We felt each one. But we loved our Queen, becaussse ssshe made usss, and ssso we continued to ssserve her.

"Then a few of my brothersss and I made plansss to

essscape her rule—we did not like killing, and we wanted a life of peassse. Ssso I and a few othersss broke with the mob of our kin, and we went off into the woodsss, to have our own livesss. Sssometimesss, I would sssee sssome of my brothersss, and sssometimesss they would be evil. Not all of usss were, not I, nor my friendsss. But Frud will gladly eat you both, given the chanssse, so hurry up and ussse that knife I sssaw you sssneak into your pantsss, sky-being, and I will help you kill Frud with your magic ssstones. But only if you promissse to leave me be."

"And why should we do that?" Anandra said, just as Iris felt the ropes around their wrists begin to give. She'd been so scared and then so captivated by the monster's tale she hadn't even noticed Anandra sawing through their ropes with her dagger. Anandra was up on her feet in no time, and she got Iris to stand behind her, seemingly ready to protect her if need be. "Why should we trust you, Kuk?"

"Becaussse, I would have killed you by now if I'd wanted to. It would have been easssy. Now, take thisss," he told Anandra, tossing her the bag that held her magic stones. Anandra caught it smoothly with her empty hand. "Frud will be back in here sssoon enough, and you ssshould be ready for him." He rose to his feet with a surprising grace, and it was then that he really seemed different from the other two monsters. Iris wasn't even sure if she could call him a monster any longer, considering how helpful and kind he seemed. *Seemed.* Because all they had were his words, and they had no true proof of his supposed honesty yet. "Here he comesss! Get ready!"

Anandra took out a stone and prepared to throw it. Seconds later, Frud came through the cave's opening. A dumbfounded expression appeared on his face when he saw Anandra and Iris standing there, untied and armed. "Why are they—"

But just then a well-placed stone hit him right in the

middle of his forehead. He fell as quickly as the first monster, Gar, had, and as gracelessly.

"Now go, and be careful," Kuk said to them. "I have a feeling that thisss land will not be sssafe for much longer. There isss word that evil is in the land, and I can feel it in my very bonesss. I can alssso feel that you two may be able to ssstop it, or I would not have ressscued you. I wasss pretty hungry, after all." And then a dry, raspy cackle rose from his thick throat. Was he *laughing*?

But before Iris could figure out if this so-called monster had a sense of humor—a somewhat sick one—he bowed to them and left the cave.

"Well, that was unexpected," Iris exclaimed, retrieving her bag from the edge of the cave. "Now, which way?"

"We have only one option, I think. We shall go deeper into the cave." Anandra reached into her bag and drew out a torch. *One that was already lit!* Would wonders never cease, Iris asked herself with a grin, and she followed Anandra away from the entrance of the cave and the deceased monster.

She almost wished they could have brought Kuk with them. He seemed kind, and with his apparent strength, he might have proved to be useful. But it looked like he didn't think so, and he probably had his own life to live. It really was intriguing, though, what he'd had to say about her and Anandra. Did they pose a threat to this evil he sensed in the land? And were his sensors even slightly accurate? She couldn't ask him, as they were now going in opposite directions, and so Iris just followed Anandra and her torch's light deeper and deeper into the cave.

After a while, Iris came to believe that they might be lost. Anandra had been pausing for a few minutes each time the path split, and by the time they reached a large, dimly lit room,

Anandra let out a large sigh and announced that they were, indeed, lost.

"It must be close to nightfall, now. Let us make camp here, and hopefully I'll be more clearheaded, and therefore able to find our way out of here, come morning." Anandra took a large blanket out of her bag and spread it out on the ground in the cave, which was quite a beautiful one, as caves went. Similar to most such places, it had the usual stalactites and stalagmites, but they were anything but common, shining and shimmering in the light from Anandra's torch, glimmering like opals, and they almost were more beautiful than Anandra was, Iris thought. Almost...

"Would you like to eat now, or should I try my luck at seducing you first?" Anandra walked over to Iris and ran her fingernails down her arm, sending slight tingles down her back.

But there was no denying it: she was damned hungry. "As much as it pains me to say this, I'm...well, actually really, really hungry. That was a lot of walking, and while I try to keep in shape, I'm not used to being on my feet all day long for so many days in a row."

"Then we must do our best to get you into better shape after dinner," Anandra announced with a mischievous grin. No question what she was talking about, Iris thought to herself as she settled down onto the blanket.

Dinner was more bread, more cheese, some wine-like drink, and a few pieces of fruit like the kind they'd eaten Iris's first morning in this world. That morning already felt like it was light-years away, and the person she'd been when she'd come to this world seemed very far away, too. The old her never would have been this brave, this risk-taking, and the old her never, ever would have done the incredibly adventurous, incredibly kinky things she'd done with Anandra each time they'd gotten naked together.

She made quick work of her dinner, because she couldn't wait for the real meal, the acts that would fully feed her body and mind. After eating, she quickly shed her clothes while a wide-eyed, appreciative-looking Anandra watched, sipping her drink and smiling softly at the sight of Iris's bare skin. Or, at least, that was what Iris hoped was causing her to smile.

"Do you know how beautiful you are?" Anandra asked quietly, taking one of Iris's wrists. She stretched Iris's arm above her head, running her other hand up and down her arm and squeezing it here and there. "Even your arms are beautiful…elegant…ideal."

"I've never been told I have nice arms before," Iris responded, feeling nervous as Anandra continued to touch her arm. How could this woman, this gorgeous woman, find *her* so attractive? It seemed unbelievable, and yet, the look that Anandra was giving her made her words seem to ring true. "Thank you," she added.

"You may thank me later, once I've done everything to your body that I plan to tonight." Anandra locked eyes with her. "Can you bring any other sexual implements into being for me? That's an order, by the way," and Anandra chuckled softly. "Yes, you must do as I say." Then Anandra yanked her arm behind her head and slammed her to the blanket. Luckily, its padding kept the ground from hurting her back, but the strong grip Anandra had on her arm hurt just a little, and she felt the strain of the position it was being pulled into, felt it deliciously. She'd already started to get aroused, so there was nothing to slow Anandra's hand when she shoved her way into Iris's cunt, fucking her with her fingers, rough and quick movements that were obviously doing the trick, from the way Iris was writhing around with each firm thrust.

"Bring me something I can put inside you, possibly something I can put into your ass while I fuck you with my fingers. I want you to be fucking full, every single hole." With those words, she shoved her tongue into Iris's mouth. She thrust it in time to each penetrating push she made into Iris's cunt with her fingers.

Iris tried to do as Anandra had ordered, but she was so distracted by her tongue and fingers that it was more challenging than it had been before. But after a few seconds more of kissing and fingers invading her body (welcomely, of course), she heard a quiet thud to her left, and they turned to see a small bottle and a line of pearlescent beads, each one bigger and bigger as they climbed up the thick bar that connected them. Iris gasped at their sudden appearance and at their increases in size. She'd never had a single thing in her ass before she'd come to this world, and now these? Could she take even the smallest one?

"And what are these, my sweet?"

"A…anal beads. You put them in your ass. And I've read that, um, if you pull them out during orgasm, it intensifies the orgasm."

"And the bottle?"

"Lube, for inserting them."

"Looks like fun." Anandra removed her fingers from Iris's cunt, leaving it sadly empty. But only a few moments later, a slicked-up bead was pressed hard against Iris's ass, slowly working its way inside, Anandra's fingers gripping it tight. Soon enough, Iris's asshole was also gripping it tight, as she felt it spread her open the slightest bit and then slide inside her. Anandra tugged at it, showing Iris how secure it was inside her, and she surprised herself (yet another surprise!) by gasping in delight at the sensation. "Someone, and by 'someone' I mean you, Iris, seems to like having her ass filled up. Maybe I should find out if that someone likes having her clit played with while she has a tiny little bead penetrating her ass."

Happily, Iris *did* enjoy having her clit played with while her ass was full, and it turned out (unsurprisingly) that she enjoyed it a little bit more with each bigger, wider, rounder bead, each one going in with ease with a slight push of Anandra's fingers. With each bead, she sped up her fingers a little, until Iris felt their pressure causing an equal amount of pressure to build within her body, until it could no longer be held in, until it had to be released.

"Are you going to come, you slut? Are you?"

"Yes...yes!" The orgasm rushed to the surface, her clit growing as hard as it ever had been, and just as the orgasm began, Anandra began to pull the beads out of her ass, one by one, and the orgasm just grew and grew as each bead slid out.

As it reached its final peak, Anandra removed her fingers from Iris's clit, shoved them into her mouth, and ordered, "Taste yourself, and don't you dare stop coming."

Iris didn't. She couldn't have, not even if she'd tried, which of course was the last thing she'd ever want to do mid-orgasm. She kept coming as the final bead left her body and as Anandra's fingers, tasting of her cunt, sweet and tart, spread her mouth wide, sliding in and out and making drool run to her lips and moisten them, making them as wet as her spasming cunt.

"Good girl, what a good girl you are." There it was, as Anandra said these words, the final touch of orgasm, and then Iris collapsed—weak, sated, and happy.

"I'll give you a few moments, and then I think I would like to try out these bead things. You seemed to enjoy them well enough, after all."

Iris caught her breath and tried to take as little time as she possibly could before she crouched between Anandra's legs and began to slide the first bead into her ass, watching it slip inside her with ease. She copied Anandra, using her fingers on her clit as only minutes ago Anandra had been doing to her, but this time, as she worked Anandra toward orgasm, her nipples got tweaked and her shoulder got bitten, and Anandra roared around her flesh as she shook beneath Iris and came, quickly, twice in a row.

As they lay down on the blanket and got ready to sleep, Iris had to ask her. "I thought you always came first. I mean, got off first. Wasn't that what you said?"

"Not always," Anandra replied in a sleepy voice. "Besides, you were looking so pretty, and I like making pretty girls happy. It's just my way."

After Anandra was asleep, Iris snuck out of bed and got her pen and notebook. She nibbled on the end of the pen for a bit, wondering where to start, and then began writing her next letter to Jane.

Dear Jane,

It feels like it's been weeks, or months, since I arrived here. I feel...I feel really different, almost like I'm not the girl, the woman you knew when we were living together. How's Billy doing, by the way? I thought it was unfair that you got to keep our cat, but you know me—there was absolutely no way I was going to put up a fight. I almost feel like I would have put up a struggle if we'd split up just now, even though I've only been here four nights, just four nights.

But I feel different, and it's not just the sexual experiences, although that part of my time here has been a change from the ordinary. I'm not shy like I used to be, either naked or clothed, and I'm no longer afraid to ask for what I want.

Which is why I think I can now easily ask you to return your hand, your body, your heart to me. If you will give me them, that is.

And...and I'll end with saying that I like it here, and I like Anandra, and while I do want to get back to you, I also...I also almost want to stay.

Iris lowered her pen after writing those words. What the heck did she write that for? Why would she want to stay here? What would she gain from it? What was here that wasn't in her world?

A soft sigh to her right and the sight of whom it came from let her know exactly why she wanted to stay here. Her grandmother Sallie sat cross-legged on the ground not far away, her silvery hair shining in the light from the torch Anandra had stabbed into the soft dirt a few feet away from their blanket.

"Sweet, darling Iris. Here I am again, and I'm damn happy to see you. Did you like the warrior's story, by the way? And have you been eating enough? You look a little thin."

"It's just all this walking," she told Sallie, and found herself smiling at the sight of one of the dearest people in the world to her.

"I'll say! You've been doing much more than your poor old granny on her wobbly legs could do. You probably won't be surprised to hear that I use a cane these days. Although it is a beaut, carved from a Sycla tree and inlaid with semiprecious stones. I wish I was half as pretty as it is!"

"Oh, Sallie, you're still beautiful to me."

"Thank you, dear. I hope Brenne would still think so."

Brenne, her grandmother's partner, had died when Iris was less than two years old. She'd gotten sick, very sick and very suddenly, and before the doctors could figure out what was ailing her, she passed. Sallie had kept many photos of the two of them scattered throughout the house. There had also been a painting of them in front of a large mansion and garden, with a carved otter statue sitting by their front porch next to some flowers Iris had never seen anywhere outside of the painting.

"Brenne would think you were more than just beautiful, Sallie. Far more."

"My, sweetie, you're going to make an old woman blush. Well, if you insist on complimenting me, I suppose I'll just have to sit here and take it." Her grandmother flashed a toothy grin at Iris, showing that she didn't seem to mind the compliments in the least. "Now, about that story…"

"The warrior you were talking about, was that Kuk?"

"Yes, it was. I once knew him well. A kind, gentle creature, only used his strength for violence when he had no other choice. Now, would you like to hear a song?" Before Iris could answer, Sallie cleared her throat and began to sing in a clear, smooth voice. Her song was about a war, one that was fought between good and evil, and about warriors fashioned of clay and then brought to life to fight the people of this world and take over for a cruel and heartless queen. A queen named Tressa, whom Iris remembered hearing about earlier. This song had to be about the Great War, and when she turned to see if her grandmother's singing had woken Anandra, she saw that she was still asleep, but a few tears were running down her face. Along with the tears was a slight smile, though, and as Iris listened to Sallie's song, she hoped that Anandra's dreams held some joy and would distract her from the hardships of her past. At least for the next few minutes. At least for tonight.

When she looked back in her grandmother's direction, the last few notes of the song escaped her lips, and then she was silent for a few seconds.

"I wish I could touch you," Iris told her, and now she was crying a little, too. "Will I ever be able to again?"

"I couldn't possibly hope for it any more than I do. But before there's a chance for that, I must tell you that I can't get to you right now. I'm trapped in another realm, and it would take a great deal of magic to bring me into the one you are in now. And...and I need to warn you about something, too."

"Oh, great." Iris crossed her arms, and her tears stopped flowing then. "I mean...I'm sorry, but it's just been really hard, much more stressful than even midterms."

Her grandmother laughed. "I would imagine so! Although I know it hasn't all been stressful, you little minx." A dramatic, teasing wink came with her words, and Iris laughed.

"I hope you haven't been watching us!"

"Oh, of course not. I just know from my days with Brenne how a woman carries herself differently, when, well...but back to what I was saying. I have a worry that something waits for you at your destination, at the castle. Something bad. Something that...oh, hell! I'm fading, pumpkin, I have to go...I'll try to visit you again tomorrow night. I have hopes that the little bit of power I was able to send to your realm will send you next to the place where I wanted you to go. Good luck! I love you!" Sallie's image flickered then, and she began to fade.

And now she was gone. Now, Iris was crying, and it took her a long hour before the tears stopped and she was able to sleep.

CHAPTER EIGHT

Iris didn't know what had woken her, but it very well could have been Anandra, because she was now up and on the move, rifling through her magic sack and looking wide-awake. "Are you scaring up some breakfast?" Iris asked her. "And does that breakfast include some cheefen?"

She'd grown to like the cheefen, and maybe she'd grown to more than just "like" it. That thought made her think about other things that she'd grown to like, if by "things" she meant "Anandra."

"Yes, there will be cheefen aplenty, I assure you of this."

"Good. Very, very good." She wanted to ask if there would be some hot sex either before or after the cheefen and breakfast were served, but when Anandra walked over to her and planted a very luscious, moist kiss on her lips, she no longer needed to ask her question. And it was answered further as Anandra cupped her breast, squeezing it a little, then a little more, until her hand was almost like a vise.

Iris made a sharp noise against Anandra's lips, and Anandra pulled back just a centimeter or so and asked, "Too much?" Her lips were practically still touching Iris's when she spoke, which struck Iris as very hot.

"Not in the least. Please, keep going!" Iris made an even

louder sound as Anandra did just that, tightening her grip on Iris's breast even more, causing her to tighten in other, lower places, to clench her cunt and wish that it was clenching down on some part of Anandra.

Her wish was soon answered, as Anandra, seeming to remember that she had a pussy as well as breasts, reached down and parted its lips, stroking her clit and then letting go of her chest. Iris gasped at the sudden release of her hand, half-relieved and half-saddened by the lack of pressure where it once had been. Anandra continued to circle her clit, adding bit by bit to the pressure of her fingers against it.

Now that her fingers were slicked up, she showed Iris that she had other plans for those fingers, other plans than just getting her off. "Get on your back," she ordered, and after a moment's hesitation, Iris did as she said. Anandra mounted Iris's face, bending down the length of her body and showing Iris that she was long enough to reach her cunt and then some. The "and then some" seemed to mean that while Iris was supposed to eat *her* out, she was apparently going to play with Iris's ass. So while Iris licked and sucked at her clit, as Iris first brought her mouth to Anandra's hot, wet clitoris, Anandra brought her finger to Iris's asshole, circling it instead of her clit, now, with firm-yet-tender strokes.

Iris moaned against her lover's cunt, and those sounds combined with her tongue's pressure seemed to bring Anandra quite close to the edge. Just as Anandra started to push the tip of her wet finger into Iris's ass, she came, bucking against Iris's lips and letting her finger slip a little farther into Iris's ass. It hurt, but just mildly, and then it hurt even less, as, still coming, Anandra started working away at Iris's clit again, working it over until Iris came too, feeling her ass clench on Anandra's finger and her cunt clench on nothing at all.

"Not...not bad." Iris panted. "Not bad at all!"

"Why, thank you, Iris. I'm happy to hear that you approve." It was now that Iris realized a tiny stream was running through their cave, and she joined Anandra in washing her hands in its water before they sat down to a small meal of cheefen and some sort of breakfast bun: it was somewhat like a cinnamon roll, only spicier and with thicker, chewier walls.

"What's this called?" Iris asked her, already halfway done with the delicious pastry before she even thought to ask.

"It's a prahl roll. Do you approve?"

"Well, my taste buds seem to. Man, is it ever good." She finished her roll and went and rinsed her hands in the stream again. "Good, but messy," she added, and Anandra laughed and nodded.

"My grandmother used to make them. These aren't as good as hers, but there's no chance of ever having one as good as hers again."

"My grandmother is a great cook, too," Iris said, thinking as she said this that in the not-too-distant past, she would have said "was" instead. But although she didn't really have definitive proof at this point, she was almost certain she should be keeping all comments about her grandmother in the present tense.

"So she's still alive? You're lucky, then. Very lucky." Anandra's face softened and, thankfully, instead of frowning and tearing up, she smiled. Iris wanted to know about her past, she realized now. She wanted to know about Anandra's parents and grandmother, whom she seemed to still care about immensely. Iris knew about loss herself, considering she'd never gotten to know her parents and had lost contact with her grandmother at such a young age. She may have loved her foster parents, but it wasn't the same with them as it had been with her grandmother. She'd always felt too different from them, always even more removed from them than merely lacking shared DNA would allow for. Almost like she was a different species than them. And maybe, now that she knew where her grandmother was truly from—this entirely different world—she could finally understand why that was.

But she couldn't tell Anandra yet, because although she liked the woman, she didn't know yet if she could trust her with this information. Her grandmother's words had worried her a bit about sharing information, and so she decided to be cautious about what she told her new friend. Because friend or not, she'd only known Anandra a mere three days, and even if this was their fourth morning together, and even if she was more than happy to share her body with her, she wasn't even close to ready to share anything more than her friendship and flesh. And could she really, truly trust Anandra? She wondered about this as they packed up their things and got ready to head out.

She also chose not to tell Anandra about what she'd found under the shirt Anandra had loaned to her as they prepared to leave the cave. Underneath the shirt lay a flower, the same as the ones in the cornflower-blue, dried bouquet her grandmother had kept in her bedroom. Only this one was fresh, softly perfumed and a much brighter blue. Had her grandmother sent it to her? She decided she believed she had, and so she slipped the flower into her pocket, wondering if perhaps it would come in handy sometime in the future.

She followed Anandra to a hall of rock at the opposite end of the cave from where they'd slept and saw the torch from the day before still burning brightly in Anandra's hand. "Do you think you have a better idea today of how to get out of the cave?" she asked her.

"I think I might," Anandra said, but she sounded anything but positive.

"Maybe I can help," said a high-pitched voice from above

them, and Iris ducked down as a large, white-and-gray shape came swooping toward her head.

The shape stopped about a foot away from Iris's face, and when she saw its true size, she got up from her crouched position, a little embarrassed that a tiny flying rat had scared her so. It wasn't even as big as her head. Instead, it was about the size of her hand, pale gray with a white chest and a bat's leathery wings, only these wings were also pale gray, with white around the edges and along each spot where the wings bent. "Name's Jaheer, and I'd like to help you get out of here."

"And why might you, strange cave creature, want to help us?" Anandra asked, sounding just as hesitant to trust the animal as her words implied.

"Because, you clearly do not belong in this cave, and because I like it better when it's calm and quiet in here. And," the rat-with-wings said, alighting on Iris's shoulder and raising its voice, "because I am the kind and generous sort, and will do anything to help a gentle-looking pair of ladies." It made a trilling sound, flapped its wings one more time, and nuzzled Iris's cheek. She couldn't help it—she made the high-pitched girly noise women like her reserved for cute animals and romantic gestures.

"Was that you, or the creature?" Anandra asked.

"Um, me." Iris's face heated up a few degrees at her question, but when Anandra grinned at her, she realized she was being teased, and she squeezed her shoulder. "Do you think we should accept its help?"

"I...I suppose we have no other choice, because it very well may have a better idea of how to get out of here than I do. I'm afraid this cave system has bested me."

"Good!" The creature sounded happy, and it made that trilling noise again. "Go forward through this hall, then! Forward, onward!"

It sounded almost too excited to be helping them, so Iris guessed it had been telling the truth when it said it enjoyed helping others. Either that, or it was going to lead them to a sharp drop and knock them over the edge with its cute little pink feet. That seemed unlikely, though, because the creature had apparently taken a liking to Iris, nuzzling her now and then as it directed them through the cave's many tunnels and rooms.

Upon reaching a large opening in the cave, leading to what looked like a tall, green hedge, the creature flew off Iris's shoulder and waved them on, flying backward and in the direction from which they'd just come. "Good luck, ladies! Good luck!"

"Strange little creature," Anandra muttered as they finally left the dark cave and entered the brightness of the outdoors once again.

"I liked it!" Iris announced. "And it seemed to have been telling the truth," she continued, as she followed Anandra through an opening in the hedge and into a lush, flowering garden.

Now inside the hedge, they were surrounded by overflowing flowerbeds, and a huge marble fountain stood in the middle of the path. Next, Iris took in the various statues all around them, each a tall, strong-looking woman or man. They all held spears or swords and shields. And after she noticed them, she realized they were beginning to move, each of them stepping down from the stands they'd been on. The statues were coming to life!

Not only were they coming to life, but they were quickly advancing on her and Anandra, brandishing their weapons, and Iris realized the two of them were clearly not welcome here.

As she turned to flee back into the cave, she noticed a

flowering bush to her left, full of bright-blue flowers identical to the one in her pocket and to the ones that had decorated Sallie's bedroom dresser. She decided then that there was only one thing to do now, and it was not turning tail and running from this beautiful garden. No, she could think of only one possible way to rescue herself and Anandra, and only she could do it. She straightened her back and cleared her throat.

Then she began to sing, the same song her grandmother had sung to her the previous night. The words and tune were shockingly easy to remember, flowing from her lips like she'd been born knowing them. Also shocking was the fact that it worked just as she'd hoped it would. The statues stopped advancing on them, and then they joined hands with one another and danced, a flowing, graceful dance like people might have done to bring a good harvest, to bring rain or sun or life to one another's land.

When the song ended, the statues stopped dancing, bowed to her and Anandra, and climbed back onto their pedestals, freezing in place and looking like solid stone once more.

"How did you do that?" Anandra's mouth was slightly agape when she first spoke, and it was still slightly open when she'd finished speaking.

Iris didn't know how to answer her, and she didn't want to tell her the truth, so she said the first lie that came to mind. "I dreamed of that song last night." It was close enough to the truth to sound true, or at least it sounded mostly true to her when she spoke those words.

"Must have been some dream! Shall we continue into the garden, then?"

"I think we should. I have a strong sense that we're going to be completely safe here for the rest of our stay." Iris kept her reason for saying this to herself; her grandmother and this garden were connected, deeply connected in some way. Had her grandmother lived here once upon a time? Had this been Sallie's home?

Any wondering about whether that was the case escaped Iris's mind as soon as she saw the picnic blanket and the retro wicker basket sitting in its center. Perfect timing, because her stomach seemed to think it was right about time for lunch.

"What's this?" Anandra was clearly suspicious, and if Iris hadn't figured out her grandmother's attachment to this place, she'd have been suspicious as well.

"I think it's fine. No, Anandra, I *know* it's fine. Please, I'm hungry, and I'd like you to trust me so we can eat." Iris started walking toward the blanket, hoping Anandra would follow suit.

"I'm hungry, too, but why should I trust whatever food is in that basket, should there be any? How do we know there isn't something dangerous inside it instead? Like a poisonous snake, or barbed arrows, or…Iris, wait!"

Anandra rushed in her direction, but it was too late. Iris had opened the basket and was no longer safe from the sandwiches, bottle of lemonade, and deviled eggs that sat inside it. Or, rather, they were no longer safe from her.

"It's fine, totally fine. Look!" And Iris tilted the basket and showed Anandra its contents.

"But how do we know the food is free of poison or magic?" She sat down and opened the glass box holding the sandwiches, then pulled a small chunk of chicken salad out from the edge of one of them. "I'll try it first. Then we'll wait thirty minutes, and if I'm not dead by then—oh my, this is delicious!"

Long before the thirty minutes were up, both of them were done with their sandwiches and had eaten a few deviled eggs and drunk a fair share of the lemonade.

"I know we still aren't sure if we're safe, but I believe that between this lovely, warm weather and our full stomachs, a brief nap is called for." Anandra yawned and lay back on the blanket, propping her face up on her hand. "Unless you have a better idea?"

"I don't. Or, actually, I do, but my 'better idea' can wait until we've slept for a few minutes. Just a few, though, because I want to finish exploring the garden and see if there's anywhere nice we can sleep for the night. I have a feeling there will be, to tell the truth." Iris lay down beside Anandra, shutting her eyes and letting her body relax in the gentle sun. A light breeze licked at her skin every now and then, but it didn't cool her too much to keep her from drifting into a sleep as delicious as the food had been.

She had no idea how much time had passed between shutting her eyes and reopening them, but the sun was clearly lower in the sky, and the first hints of twilight made the purple and blue flowers in the garden glow slightly. Anandra's stars were lighting up a little too, just like they seemed to during every dusk, apparently doing what they could to match the actual night sky. But it was at least a few hours before true dark, which meant they would have more than enough sun left for what Iris wanted to do next. She shut her eyes and held out her hand, and when she looked at it again, it held some scary-looking nipple clamps and a ball gag.

"Hey, Anandra, check these out!" she announced, and Anandra awoke, shoving herself upright and glancing around.

"What? Huh? Are you all right, Iris?"

"I'm more than all right. Look!" She held out the two items for Anandra to inspect, who took the nipple clamps into her hands and examined them, and then did the same with the ball gag.

"What does each one do?" she asked Iris, and if Iris hadn't

known better, she'd have thought Anandra sounded a little proud of her. Maybe she was. Iris was proud of herself, after all. It hadn't been that long since she had to get sex toys the old-fashioned way, although on Earth, she only owned a single vibrator and a small bottle of lube.

"The metal ones are something known as 'nipple clamps,' and I'm guessing you can figure out what they do. And the other one is a ball gag. You attach the straps behind someone's head and place the ball between their lips."

"I was hoping I would get to gag you at some point, although I've always just used spare strips of cloth." Always? Damn it, Iris thought, she did *not* want to think of Anandra's sexual past. It had started to seem like she'd had more than her fair share of partners, which was something Iris didn't want think about for a second.

"I've heard a ball gag works much better," she told Anandra, hoping that her knowledge of Earth's sex toys might win her some points and push her standing beyond those other lovers. "And they look much hotter than a strip of cloth, too. I've seen pictures of women using them that have really turned me on."

"Well, let's make what you've seen in the past become a reality for you. Open wide, my little slut. Open up for me…" Iris did, and Anandra placed the black rubber ball between her lips, wrapping the straps around her head and then buckling it in place. Iris had never had her mouth held wide-open like this during sex before. Would it do something for her the way the photos had? Looking at hot, gagged women was one thing, but being one of those women was entirely another.

She didn't have much time to think about whether it turned her on, though, because Anandra yanked up her shirt and bra, revealing her breasts to the cooling afternoon air. Iris shivered just a little, which was possibly what caused Anandra's sudden smile to appear. She bit her bottom lip and then pinched open one of the clamps and placed it around Iris's right nipple, which had been made hard by the slightly chilly air. And it just might have had some help from her growing arousal.

She didn't have much time to consider this, though, because now she had to do her best to not cry out in pain as Anandra let go of the clamp and it attached itself to her nipple, a muffled gasp leaving her lips instead. Instead of crying out when the second one was attached only moments later, she writhed around on the blanket as it pinched down on her skin and moaned around the gag. It seemed like gags and nipple clamps were more than just fun to look at on other women; it seemed like they were more than just fun for Iris, too.

It was much more than just fun to feel her mouth spread wide open; more than just fun to feel a bit of saliva pool in her mouth and make her lips as wet as her cunt; more than just fun to have the clamps pinch down on her nipples and bring heat to her chest like she'd never felt before.

She arched her back when Anandra pulled on the chain, but the sounds she made were only half from the pain it caused, or maybe even less than half. The second yank of the chain caused much more pleasure than pain, and the third time she pulled on it—much harder than the first two times—it was hardly unpleasant at all, sending blissful tingles up and down her bare skin, dancing across it like the heat of desire.

Desire was something that Iris felt strongly now, and she remembered the safeword for when she was gagged. She grunted three times, and Anandra quickly removed the gag.

"Are you all right? Was that too much?"

Iris panted for a few seconds, then swallowed the saliva that had filled her mouth. "No, of course not. Not at all. But I wanted to get you off, and I wanted to be able to do so with my mouth."

"But if you use your mouth, I won't be able to play with your tits and these nipple clamps while you do so. And wouldn't that be a complete and utter shame?" Anandra's eyes made it clear that there was only one possible answer to her seemingly rhetorical question.

"Of course it would...ma'am."

"Now that's what I like to hear! Get to work, then." Anandra wrapped her fist around the chain, her grip on it more than solid, and Iris reached down and unbuttoned her lover's pants. She shoved her hand deep inside them and found her way to Anandra's clit. It was quite engorged, and slick with Anandra's juices. She began to rub at it, feeling a little pride that she knew what Anandra needed to get off by now, and knew it well.

It didn't take long before Anandra was thrusting her whole body against Iris, her muscles tight and her cunt wetter than ever as she came. But that wasn't all that happened: something far more shocking than that occurred when Anandra yanked the hardest she had so far on Iris's chain.

Iris's own cunt grew tight and wet as the chain pulled at her nipples, and then she came, too, pressing her body as tight against Anandra's as Anandra had pressed her own against Iris's. She was coming hard, and just from some mere nipple pain! Although "mere" might not have been the right word, because as her orgasm ended, she yelped in pain. "Ouch!"

Anandra quickly removed each clamp, causing two more cries of "ouch!" to leave Iris's mouth. "Too much, I guess?" Anandra asked with a goofy, lopsided grin. "*Finally* too much?"

"Oh, yeah. It really was." Iris took a few seconds to lightly massage her tender nipples.

"So you have limits after all. I was starting to wonder. But did I...did I actually bring you to orgasm with just a pull of that chain?"

"A very strong pull of it! And yes, you did. I can't...I can't believe it myself. I used to have such a hard time coming with my ex, and she seemed to think it was all my fault. But I'm starting to wonder if she was wrong."

"I think she was more than merely wrong, Iris. You're amazingly orgasmic, if you can get off merely from what I just did to your poor nipples."

"I just can't believe it," Iris repeated in a soft, awe-filled voice. "I just can't."

"Believe it or not, it's getting cold out here. We should get our clothing back in place and find somewhere to spend the night."

Anandra rebuttoned her pants and Iris fixed her bra and shirt. Much better, she thought, and then she realized that wasn't true in the least. Much better had been when she was pressed up against Anandra, her strong, luscious body keeping Iris warm in the slightly chilly air, so divine against Iris's. *So very divine.*

But they couldn't have stayed out there all night, not with how cold the air was growing, with the sun now falling beneath the top of the hedge surrounding the garden, and so Iris followed Anandra through a row of what looked like red and blue roses, choosing to let her friend lead the way. They reached a part of the path that went down a slight hill, and at its base sat something surprisingly familiar to Iris.

Upon seeing the familiar sight, she thought of the painting her grandmother Sallie had hanging on the wall in her bedroom: the one of her, Brenne, and an otter statue, right in front of a mansion. There may have been no Sallie and Brenne waiting for her on the mansion's steps, but this was without a doubt the exact same place, complete with the same flowers near its porch, the ones Iris had never seen before in real life. Her grandmother had told her they were very rare, but perhaps that was just because they were nonexistent on Earth. They clearly existed here, though.

Yes, the mansion from the painting was actually real. Iris wondered if the stone otters would also be here, the ones whom her grandmother had spun tales about. Tales that very well could have been truth and not fiction as she had always thought.

The mansion below them was peach-colored and two-storied, with a sloping roof covered with large, darker-peach tiles. It had tall and narrow arched windows and a shaded porch, with chaise lounges and tables on each side of the front door. Iris couldn't wait to get inside, not because of the oncoming night, but because she just had to know what her grandmother's mansion contained. Because it had to be her grandmother's mansion, she thought, as she descended the hill. Between the song that had saved them from the attacking statues and the painting she'd looked at many times throughout her life, not to mention the familiar blue flowers from Sallie's dresser, it couldn't have been anything else but her grandmother's old home.

Would she find Sallie here, though, or would she only find echoes of her grandmother's past? There was only one way to find out. She walked the rest of the way down the hill, Anandra following close behind, and approached the mansion's front door. It was unlocked, and so she turned the silver knob and stepped inside.

CHAPTER NINE

Iris had only seen this mansion from the outside, so nothing about its entryway was familiar, nor should it have been. Still, she had a feeling—a powerful sense—that she'd been here before, if only for a day or two. Not that this sense *made* sense, but it definitely was there, strong and undeniable.

Vases of dried flowers sat on each of the entryway's tables, in shades of blue, violet, and pink, all obviously from the garden they'd just left. The very last of the afternoon's sun wasn't needed to light the hall, because round, pearl-shaded wall sconces were placed every few feet or so, their warm glow lending an air of comfort to the place. A painting hung on the wall at the end of the entryway, where there were two hallways, one going off to the left, the other to the right. The painting was of a woman who was just as familiar to Iris as the mansion, a woman whom she'd mostly just seen in pictures— her grandmother's deceased partner, Brenne.

She looked quite young in the painting, and a large gold lion sat at her feet. Both Brenne and the lion looked proud, but kindness shone in each set of eyes, too, clear enough for anyone to be able to see it. Her grandmother had always told her how kind Brenne had been to her, and it was nice to see that goodness preserved in such a beautiful piece of artwork.

Apparently, her grandmother's skill at painting could have been called "otherworldly" in both senses of the word.

"You're spending a long time looking at that painting," Anandra said. Her voice made Iris jump a little, because she'd been so lost in thought.

"It's just...it's just very realistic is all. Very good work."

"Indeed it is. But we should continue. I want to make sure no surprises are waiting for us in here, like those dangerous statues. Who knows what else might be guarding this place from intruders, and you can't spend all night singing that song you stilled the statues with. As beautiful as it was, and as skilled a singer as you are, I still want both of us to be able to sleep soundly tonight. Tomorrow, we'll need to find our way out of here and back in the right direction. Although I wasn't planning to come to this place, wherever it is," and here she cupped Iris's elbow and began to lead her away from the painting, "it will do quite well as somewhere to spend the night, especially if we find some more delicious food prepared for dinner. Those sandwiches were scrumptious, and I look forward to seeing what else we might get to dine on while we're here."

Iris allowed Anandra to lead her down the hallway to the left of the painting, where she began to hear what sounded like a small waterfall. And that was exactly what it was, because at the end of the hallway, and through a door Anandra insisted on walking through first, was the most incredible swimming pool Iris had ever seen.

Its waters were an enticing aquamarine, and it had to be Olympic-sized, or at least close. A few lounge chairs sat along its edges, and the front of the room was where the waterfall-like sounds had come from, where a very natural-looking artificial waterfall fed into a small, round pool that in turn flowed into the much larger one. Iris approached, staring down into the clear water and taking in the turquoise and lapis mosaics that decorated its walls and floor. "Do you like skinny-dipping?" she asked Anandra. But instead of waiting for an answer, she started to remove her clothes.

"Skinny-dipping? Is that what you call swimming in the nude? I do, yes, and although I don't really advise taking off all our clothing and leaving my weapon out of reach, it seems like there's no way I'll talk you out of getting into that water. And…it seems like there's no way you'll enjoy yourself enough if you don't have a swimming partner. After all," and with these words Anandra arched one of her snow-white brows, "I don't know how good a swimmer you are, and after your previous dip in the water, I'm guessing you may wind up needing mouth-to-mouth."

"I'm not *that* bad of a swimmer, you'll see!" Iris was completely naked now, and so she stepped to the edge of the swimming pool, judged the depth of the water adequate, and dove in, surfacing a few yards away. "Mmm, the water's warm and silky. And it smells like flowers!"

"Are you sure it's not you who's perfuming the water?" Anandra looked pleased at her compliment. Either that or she was pleased to see Iris naked again, which Iris thought seemed more likely, albeit still surprising. Jane had almost never told her she was good-looking, and she'd never really told her she was more than slightly above passable, and so Iris had taken to believing she wasn't especially attractive. But Anandra had never hesitated to compliment her looks, starting right when they'd first met, so maybe she wasn't that bad after all.

Anandra dove in near where Iris had entered the water. Anandra was *far* from bad looking, Iris thought, and this was especially obvious to Iris as her friend's well-muscled, lanky form cut through the water like a knife. She broke through the surface only a few inches away from where Iris was swimming in place, the water's sudden displacement sending slight ripples off from her cresting head. Anandra closed the distance between them and gave Iris a long, deep kiss, her mouth as moist and warm as the water that surrounded them, her lips' pressure against Iris's causing even more wetness to caress her bare skin.

She couldn't possibly have been happier right then, and Jane wasn't even the one in her arms. It was strange, but thoughts of Jane and her love for her had started to fade while she'd been in this new world. Maybe her therapist had been right. Maybe she did need to put an ocean between herself and Jane to get over her...an ocean, and a universe. Well, if that was what it took to finally get over her ex, then so be it. And if what it took was letting Anandra slowly move them over to the waterfall and smaller pool as she kissed her, Iris decided that would have to be fine, too. She wasn't about to start putting up a fight now, not with the pressure of the waterfall on her back and the pressure of Anandra's lips on her front, lips that were more than welcome to keep up what they were doing for as long as her friend wanted.

As Anandra kissed her, she guided her closer and closer to the waterfall, until they were standing in front of it, the water knocking Iris slightly off balance as it rushed around her legs. Anandra didn't seem to be experiencing the same trouble, though, both her legs and her hands firm against Iris, firm and controlling her every move. Anandra pulled her arms behind her back, knocking her even more off balance, and gripped her wrists in her left hand, then nibbled her way down Iris's neck.

She led Iris over to the edge of the smaller pool and sat her on its rim, the water lapping against her lower legs as Anandra scrunched down low and proceeded to begin lapping at her cunt. Her mouth was even warmer than the water, and her tongue even silkier, and Iris didn't have enough time to be surprised that, for the second time, she was getting off first, because now she *was* getting off, her cries echoing through the tall, glowing room.

Glowing? Had it been doing that a few minutes ago? And then Iris realized that Anandra and she were lighting up the room, and not only that, but she was levitating above the water, and so was Anandra. That thought seemed to bring them crashing back down to the water as quickly as the orgasm had swept her up into the air.

Luckily, they landed fully in the water, as they apparently had traveled a few feet toward the center of the pool. Iris came up sputtering, having swallowed a little of the water on her way to the surface. She coughed a few times, and Anandra grabbed her and pulled her over to shallower waters where she could stand once more.

"You really can't swim, can you?" Anandra was clearly joking, but she also looked a little shell-shocked, which was pretty much how Iris felt, only she felt so more than just a little.

"What the hell just happened?" Iris coughed again as she made her way to the edge of the pool, where tiled steps led to a stack of white towels next to an otter statue standing on its hind legs. "And where did the statue and the towels come from? They weren't here when we came into the room." The otter statue opened its mouth. Statues weren't supposed to do that, but after her experience with the ones in the garden, she half expected it to pounce on her and then try to bite her to death with its sharp little teeth.

Instead of advancing on her, it laughed, a high, cheery tittering sound, just as she'd always imagined the otters in her grandmother's stories would sound when they found something funny. "I mean you no harm, miss," the otter said, its voice as adorable as its laugh. "My name is Tira, and I was only supposed to lead you to the dining hall, where dinner awaits you both. But at the sight of you crashing into the water, I must say, I have not had such a good laugh since the mistress of the house left us all behind."

The mistress of the house? Would that have been Sallie, Iris wondered? Or perhaps Brenne?

"She may have had a queenly manner about doing things, but she was a delightful woman. As was her daughter, if I do say so. Both of them as beautiful as you are, friend." The otter was speaking to Iris when she said these words, and Iris could think of far worse beings to be instant friends with than an adorable talking otter. But the mistress's *daughter*? Would that have been Iris's mom?

All these questions would have to wait, though, because apparently it was now time to head to the dining hall. Iris tried not to feel shy once it sank in that she was naked in front of a complete stranger, but then again, the otter was naked, too, and she didn't seem embarrassed in the least. Iris decided that it didn't matter to an otter whether you were wearing clothes or not, even if the otter happened to speak in her tongue rather than in squeaks and barks as she'd heard them do in nature. As much of the natural world as she had walked through and looked at in this new land, its version of "natural" was nothing like what Iris was used to. This fact obviously included talking otter statues.

Many questions were coming to her as she dried off and put her clothes back on, wringing out her hair in the fluffy towel she hoped the otter hadn't brought. She just had to ask. "Did you bring the towels?"

The otter smiled and shook her head. "Oh, no, miss! I only entered the room when I saw the glow coming from through the door. I realized that you and your lady-friend would want some privacy, based on the way I saw you eyeing each other on the way into the swimming hall. The towels, mind you, are magically generated when the room senses the pool is being used. It even brings towels when the other staff and I go swimming. Imagine that, us animal statues wanting to use a towel."

Iris could imagine it about as well as she could imagine a statue not sinking to the bottom of the pool. But otters were very good swimmers, or at least the version of them in her world tended to be, so, "What's for dinner?" she asked. It was time to stop thinking up questions and start thinking about food instead, Iris had decided. She could smell something delicious even through the door to the swimming hall, as the otter had called it, something juicy and meaty, something she couldn't wait to sink her teeth into. The food in this world had proved to be exceptionally tasty, she thought, and its excellence didn't seem like it would start faltering tonight, at least by the current smell of things.

Now dressed again, and almost entirely dry save her hair, she followed an also-clothed Anandra and the naked (as was natural) otter out of the room and back down the hall they'd just used to get to the pool. They took two lefts and then entered a candlelit room through a large wooden arch, where a long black table with a pristine white runner, surrounded by chairs filled with otters, positively overflowed with food. Iris was surprised that she *wasn't* surprised to see the otters with napkins in their laps and a few of them holding their forks and knives in anticipation.

"The lady of the house always insisted we dine with her," the otter told them, "and so we hoped you wouldn't mind if we did the same with you."

"No, no, not at all, especially with all that delicious food, which is clearly too much for just Anandra and me."

"Anandra, so that is your name. A pleasure to meet you, miss!" The otter made a small curtsy, pretending to lift imaginary skirts, and Iris couldn't help picturing how cute this otter might have looked in a gown and tiara. Not that she really needed any help in the cuteness category, Iris realized, and besides, if she wanted to wear such things, the otter would already be wearing them. She judged her thought to be a mite rude and decided to help her conscience by thanking the otters for the feast that lay before them all. "I can't thank you enough for your hospitality. Did you prepare the picnic as well?"

"Yes, the sandwiches were our creator's recipe. She was a very good cook, even though it wasn't what she was born to do."

"Yes, she was," Iris said softly. But when Anandra turned and asked her what she'd just said, Iris told her, "I didn't say anything. Now, how about we offer some sort of grace and then eat?"

"I could have sworn...maybe I have some water in my ears, from that sudden crash under the pool's surface. Yes, let's eat. And grace? What is that?" Anandra slid into one of the empty chairs, and Iris sat down in the one next to her.

"It's a human custom, usually religious, although I always thank Gaia instead of God."

"Gaia? Who's she?" a male otter to Iris's right asked.

"That's our word for the planet we live on, Mother Earth, the goddess of life and all of that."

"How interesting," he said, and the other otters all nodded in agreement.

"Should I thank her, then?"

"Yes, yes!" cried the otters, and so Iris took Anandra's hand in her left and the otter's slightly warm stone paw in her right.

Iris bowed her head and shut her eyes. "Gaia, we ask for

your blessings on the food you have gifted us with. May it bring all of us the strength of the earth, your strength, and we offer many thanks for your generosity."

"Hear, hear!" said a few of the otters, and others made a chirping sound that seemed to contain immense approval.

"I'm pleased you liked it," she said, feeling glad she'd made them all so happy. She was very happy, too, the happiest she'd been in quite a while; she was the happiest she'd been since Jane had dumped her. "Let's eat, then!"

Food was passed around, and Iris's plate was soon piled with a fresh, crisp salad, some sort of herb-coated, cheese-stuffed white meat, and a delicious, creamy orange mash, which tasted like a buttery mixture of carrots and sweet potatoes, two of her favorite foods. Too bad she couldn't take a freezer of these fruits and vegetables back with her to Earth, she thought as she took seconds of the mash.

They also had a very lovely, pale-pink alcohol that went perfectly with the food, tasting slightly sweet and full-bodied and just a little tart. It made Iris think of fresh lemonade spiked with some sort of incredibly high-quality, honey-flavored liquor. It was strong, though, and so despite her tongue's ardent pleading, she turned down a second serving, instead choosing some iced water that the otters were drinking instead of the alcoholic beverage. Smarter than me, those otters, she thought, as she was feeling slightly tipsy after only one glass of the lemony drink.

Nothing in the meal proved to be drugged the way Anandra had suggested earlier that day, unless Iris counted the effects of an overly stuffed stomach and the touch of fuzziness in her head from the alcohol. She'd already felt very trusting toward the otters, though, especially since it had seemed that they all cared deeply about her grandmother. Her grandmother and her mother, too, from the sounds of it. Did that mean her father had lived here as well? She didn't feel comfortable asking any of these questions in front of Anandra, not yet, at least. She knew she should have trusted her friend a little more than she realized she did at this moment in time. But…once burned, she told herself.

Yes, she had been burned the last time she'd let someone close too fast, and she was finally realizing that hadn't been her fault, that she'd just chosen the wrong person to let get so very close to her. Still, it was perfectly possible to make that mistake again, and besides, she probably wouldn't be in this world much longer, especially if they could find their way from her grandmother's estate to the castle with enough ease.

But tonight, she would just let herself enjoy Anandra's company as fully as possible. Her company and that of the otters, each of them incredibly full of personality and joie de vivre.

The otters insisted on performing what they told them was one of their last mistress's favorite plays, one called *The Lady of the Woods*. It was about a woman who rescued a young animal from a trap that a hunter had set. A little later on, the woman fell in love with the hunter, and she managed to change him from a man of violence to one of good deeds and much kindness. At the end of the play, he fell sick, then died, refusing to let his wife kill an endangered creature whose flesh was the only thing that could cure him. Iris was crying by the end of his death scene, the hunter played by a large male otter with the skills of a true thespian. His wife was played by Tira, who also did an excellent job sobbing and telling him she would always love him as he shut his eyes for the final time.

Even Anandra seemed touched by the play's ending, applauding loudly after trying to subtly wipe a few tears from her eyes when she probably thought Iris wasn't watching. Upon noticing Iris's look of concern, she turned to her and said, "My eyes are just watering. I think it's from all the flowers in this room."

"The *dried* flowers?" Iris asked, nudging her with her elbow. Then she pecked her on the cheek. "I think it's sweet that you were touched. I was, too, very much. The lady of this house, whoever she was, seems to have had good taste in plays."

"This is the first one I've ever seen. We didn't have very many artists in my village when I was young, and we had even fewer after the war." For once, Anandra didn't seem like she was going to fall apart after the word "war" came up. Was that because of what had happened the previous day, when she'd held Anandra while she cried? Was Anandra opening up now and softening around the edges? Iris had noticed the way she seemed to keep her at an arm's length, at least when they weren't having sex, and she admitted to herself now that she'd been doing the same thing. It wasn't that Anandra couldn't be trusted—she'd more than proved that by now! It was that Jane had taken away Iris's ability to trust. Good riddance, she thought for the very first time. Her therapist had been right, after all, telling her all those times that Jane had been an unskillful decision in terms of choosing people to date, and her therapist had also been right about it being time to move on.

If only her next sexual partner hadn't been someone in a magical, far-away universe that Iris didn't belong in. If only her next partner hadn't been Anandra. But when Anandra took her hand and held it tight as Tira and another otter led them to their bedroom for the night, she decided that Anandra wasn't that bad a choice. No, she wasn't a bad choice at all.

And it was definitely a *good* choice for Iris to let Anandra order her to bring them a dildo (a large one, she insisted) once they were stripped of their clothes, the room lit with a few lamps and Anandra's glowing stars. Iris took in their flickering light, almost feeling warmed by each one of them as Anandra pressed them against her.

Iris called the dildo into her hand, and she closed her fist around it when it arrived, pale purple and almost as big around as her wrist. However, it might have just been that its size and its heft had intimidated her. Because she knew it was going to be used on her, on her cunt at the very least, and so although her cunt grew wet in anticipation, she also felt it tighten and tense a bit, too, almost like it didn't know if it was really ready to be entered by something possessing such a startling circumference.

"Are you sure it'll fit?" she joked, but her voice shook a little as the words came out, betraying her nervousness.

"I'm positive. Don't worry. I'll make more than certain that it won't hurt. It wouldn't be very fun for me to stuff you full of dildo if it did, now would it?"

"That's good to hear. No, that's great to hear! I'm ready," she added, climbing onto the bed and spreading her thighs, knees bent, pussy exposed and ready to be penetrated by the dildo.

She wasn't sure she was big on bigger dildos, having had little experience with anything larger around than a few fingers before she'd come to this world, but something about the size of the dildo that Anandra was now rubbing against her cunt's opening excited her more than she'd expected it could. How would it feel, to be spread open that wide? She couldn't wait to find out.

But Anandra had decided to tease her, apparently, only pushing the dildo in mere centimeters and then right back out. She put it in only the same amount the second time, and almost less the third.

"More, please, more—I can take it." Iris moaned. It might have been quite the tease, but it was a very arousing tease… very arousing, indeed.

"You can?" Anandra stared down at her, clearly willing to shove more of it inside Iris, but only if Iris was capable of convincing her of her ability to handle its girth.

"Yes, I can. Please…please!"

Anandra moved the dildo back inside Iris at her insistence, this time pushing it in at least a few inches, spreading her wide and causing her cunt to feel almost overpowered with the intensity of it. It wasn't too much, not yet, at least, although it came close when Anandra began to fuck her with the dildo, at a leisurely pace, like she had all the time in the world to make sure she fucked Iris just right, just…exactly…right.

And just right it was, because soon enough, Iris felt herself becoming wild, almost feral, from the slowly growing ripples of sensation spreading from her cunt to her thighs, and then even farther. Was Anandra going to let her come first again, she hoped?

No, she wasn't, because only moments before Iris was positive she would have come from just a little pressure on her clit, Anandra removed the dildo and shoved it into Iris's mouth instead.

"Taste yourself, sweetheart, taste your sweet, wet goodness." And while the dildo was in Iris's mouth, *then, finally then*! her clit was given attention, Anandra's fingers rubbing it good and hard, until Iris started to—

But no, it was not to be, apparently, because just as she began reaching the height of pleasure, Anandra stopped, removed the dildo, and mounted her face. "You may come," Anandra told her, "if you get me off at the same time. Go ahead. Go ahead and use your hand, Iris. I want you to."

So Iris did, rubbing away at her clitoris as she ate out

Anandra, licking and rubbing at equally fast speeds, only slowing down her fingers and not her tongue when she worried that she was going to come before Anandra was able to. She got close again, so close, and then she could tell, by the sounds Anandra was making and by the way that her body was tightening, that she was almost there as well. So Iris let her tongue take over, let it send words of passion deep into Anandra as it did what it needed to do to get her off, let it speak the language of sex, of arousal, and she tried to speak this language as if it were her native tongue.

"Fuck, fuck!" Anandra cried out, and then she came, and Iris finally got off too, the intensity from Anandra's orgasm almost making her ignore, or forget about, her own. But that would have been impossible, because it was damn good as orgasms went, and Iris moaned and cried out against her partner's cunt, her sounds vibrating against Anandra's pussy in what she hoped was a very pleasurable way.

It seemed as if it had been, because Anandra did a mock bow when she climbed off Iris's face. "My sweet, you have done well. Very well. One might almost say ex*tremely* well, if they were to be so bold."

"Thank you. I'm glad you got your money's worth."

"But I did not pay you! I gladly would, though, if your services weren't free."

"It's just a saying in my country," Iris told her, relaxing against the sheets. Anandra caressed her side, then leaned down and kissed her for a few seconds. "Are you implying that you want to fuck again?" Iris asked her when she began to pull away. "Because I'm afraid I just don't have it in me. Give me an hour, though…"

Which is exactly what Anandra did. They talked about Iris's world while they waited for her to get her strength back, and Iris opened up, telling her about her ex and how Anandra had been really good for her self-esteem, even telling her how she'd helped Iris move on. Anandra looked shy, perhaps, when Iris told her this, only saying that she was glad to help her, and she hoped she could help her some more before it was time for her to leave.

Because, of course, Iris wasn't staying here.

After they'd each had one more glorious orgasm apiece, Iris lay down and waited for Anandra to sleep so she could write this night's letter. Would her grandmother visit her again tonight? It seemed likely, because they were staying in what had been her home at one point. Her home, and, it sounded like, Iris's mother's home, too. Was her mother still alive, like Sallie? And her father? Iris would have to ask her about that if she saw her tonight.

Once she heard Anandra's now-familiar snores, which she'd taken to thinking of as cute, she got out her notebook and pen and wrote the next letter.

Dear Jane,

I couldn't be happier that I took this trip, nor could I be happier that I'm in Anandra's world, and not my own. It's been an educational experience, full of new things and new experiences galore. I feel like I've grown even more over the last day, and there's one thing I know now, one thing I now know completely: I'm finally getting over you for good. I can finally see the mistake I made in dating you, and in staying with you for so long, and in pining over you for the year we've been broken up. Anandra has been the reason for that, and so I will be eternally grateful for this gift she's given me.

She's really an amazing person, much more than you ever were. Kind, smart, resourceful, and mind-

*blowing in bed. I really have grown to care for her. I
almost feel as if I more than care for her. I almost feel
like I'm falling in...*

And there Iris stopped writing mid-sentence. It couldn't
be true, could it? No, she wouldn't let it be true. Because even
if she was falling for Anandra, she wouldn't be moving here
or anything. She belonged on Earth, at her college and in her
town. She belonged in Jane's world. Maybe not in her life, but
that was her home, not this place. Not this world. She started
to put her notebook back into her bag, and then she heard a
voice from out in the hall.

"Come here, sweetie. I want to give you the grand tour."

It was Sallie's voice! A more welcome distraction from
her emotional conundrum couldn't have been possible. Iris
tiptoed to the door and slipped out of the room, shutting the
door behind her as quietly as she could.

There was Sallie, grinning at her, and she reached out one
of her spectral hands, running it across Iris's cheek. "My dear,
welcome to what was once your home. And mine. And your
mother's."

"*I* lived here?" Iris was surprised, but not overly so,
because a part of her had expected to hear that at some point.
"How old was I when we left?"

"I would say not much older than four months. Your
mother and Brenne and I moved into your grandfather's inn
then, a number of miles from here, to be more inconspicuous,
because that was when the Great War occurred. That was
when Tressa tried to take over this land and, thankfully, failed.
And shortly after that, you and I and Brenne went to Earth,
where Brenne's strong attachment to this world made her
unable to survive past our first year in the United States. I was
devastated, of course, but I still had you, and you more than

made up for that great loss. Come, I have much I want to show you. Follow me."

Sallie took off down the hall and drifted through a door about ten steps down from the room where Anandra was hopefully still fast asleep. Iris followed her past that door, into a room that turned out to be a heck of a lot bigger than Iris had expected, a room that contained the most amazing library Iris had ever seen. The walls formed a half circle, and it had at least five floors, with a set of stairs leading to a balcony for each set of shelves and the many books that filled them. A large number of the books had gold, silver, or copper embossing on their spines, the metallic words glittering in the candlelight from the candelabras placed at even intervals around the room. Iris noticed a quiet, repetitive sound coming from the ground floor and saw an otter. It sat at a table in the room, snoring softly with a slight whistle, its head resting on a thin book.

"We must be quiet," her grandmother whispered. "Wouldn't want to wake Eldrem."

"You must know all of their names, I would guess," Iris whispered back, and Sallie nodded.

"Each and every one of the otters is different and equally dear to me. I made them, you know, but I wanted them to develop their own personalities, so I left them all mostly blank in that area. And just look at how well they all managed to turn out." Sallie looked proud, clearly very happy with the delightful mammalian consorts she'd lived with at this mansion.

"I remember how much Brenne loved to read. Our library was never as large as this one, though."

"No, in your current world, we didn't have the resources she and I had here. We were both very wealthy, I must admit. In gold, in magic, and in family and love. Your mother and father were very much in love with each other, too, and they were ecstatic and then some when you were born, pumpkin.

They invited many, many friends to our party after you came into our lives. You were quite the prize! Still are, too. And sweetie, I am so, so sad that we've had to be apart all these years. I still don't know what has brought you back, though, and I don't know why I'm able to see you so easily, either. I wish I could see you in person. I wish—" Sallie's head shot to the right, and her eyes went wide in fear. "Oh, shit!"

Iris would have laughed at her sudden and emphatic swearing, but her grandmother didn't swear often, instead preferring playful colloquialisms, so she knew instantly that something was up, and it likely was a "something" that wasn't good.

"Get your friend," Sallie ordered her, turning back to Iris. "The statues can hold off our just-arrived intruders, but for how long I have no clue, so hurry, hurry and run. Wake up Eldrem, and he'll lead you out of here as safely as he's able. And be quick, before it's too late!"

Iris rushed over to the sleeping otter named Eldrem, who already seemed like he was rousing from his deep sleep. "Whu…" He turned his bright, beady eyes toward Iris, reaching up a paw to wipe at one of them. "Is something happening, miss? I have a feeling something is. Something dreadful, most likely. Ah, and I was having such a nice dream. The salmon were spawning."

"Something *is* wrong, and Anandra and I need your help, desperately. My grandmother was just here, or at least her projection was, and she said that trouble of some sort is here and we'll need your help to be led out of the mansion as safely as possible." Iris found she was still whispering despite the fact that the otter was now awake, but maybe her decision to speak quietly came from whatever threat awaited them outside the mansion's walls. Whatever it was, she wanted to get away from it as quickly as her feet could move.

"Right, miss. I'll be happy to oblige you. Get your friend and your things, and I'll lead you to the hidden passage." He leapt down from his chair, brushed off his paws on his hips, and trotted at a fast pace to the door, which he swung wide open with a turn of its knob and a hard shove.

"I'll be right back!" Iris ran back to the room where she and Anandra had been supposed to sleep that night. Ah, if only she *could* sleep right now, instead of having to flee from whatever danger happened to be waiting for them outside her grandmother's former home. She wanted to stay longer, to explore the place…and she wanted her grandmother to come back and tell her more about her parents' and her grandmother's true selves.

Clearly, though, she didn't have time for any of that. So Iris slammed open the door to the room she'd just been in with Anandra, where her friend was already awake and standing. The room was dark, with only a dim glow from her stars showing Iris where she was. She appeared to have just been looking out the room's window, and Iris now glanced there, too. Through the glass, she saw the outlines of dark, tall, humanoid shapes fighting other tall and humanoid shapes. Some of them had glowing red eyes, and some of them had glowing white ones. She guessed, based on what she knew of mythology and horror movies, that the red-eyed ones were the threat to her and Anandra. And there were also dark shapes that looked as if they were swords and shields held by the white-eyed shapes. These beings were most likely the statues from the previous day.

All these thoughts flitted through her head in the few seconds it took Anandra to turn to her and ask in a tense tone, "What's going on out there? Do you know?"

"There's too much to explain it all right now," she told Anandra, striding over to her bag and scooping it up. "The short version is that my grandmother, who disappeared when I was ten and who raised me until then, seems to be from this world. She's been visiting me in a kind of spectral form and—"

"Why didn't you tell me?" Anandra sounded hurt, and Iris couldn't blame her. Anandra, too, grabbed her bag, which, thankfully, was already packed. "Never mind. Tell me what you know of what's going on out there instead."

"My grandmother didn't know, just that we were under attack, and one of the otters, Eldrem, is going to lead us out the back way, so we can get away safely. Is that all right with you?"

"Do you mean to ask me if I trust you? The answer is yes, I do. Let's go!"

They left the bedroom and met Eldrem in the hall, who was wringing his paws and tapping his foot. "We have no time to waste, ladies. No time!" He gestured down the hall from them. "Follow me, and follow close, or you may lose me." With that, he got down on all fours, scampering ahead of them at a very fast pace.

They followed just behind, as he turned left at the end of the hall and then right, and then went through a large black door and down about twenty steps, into what looked like the food cellar of the mansion. It was full of baskets of fruit, hanging root vegetables, jars and bottles in many different colors, and it smelled moist, like a fresh rain.

"Go out through there," he told them, pointing toward a fringed black curtain in the back of the cellar. "It will lead you where you need to go, I promise. We can hold them off here, because those statues never lose a fight. And my, but the warriors seem to be back, or at least re-animated, re-created. I hope there are not as many of them as there were in the Great War."

"I also hope so. For *their* sake." Anandra's voice was so full of fiery rage it almost singed Iris's neck. She clearly hated anything to do with the Great War, and who could blame her? Iris couldn't, not even slightly.

"I hope so, too." Iris reached back and gave Anandra's arm a squeeze, which got her a tight smile in return. Better than no smile at all, she thought.

She was to go through the curtain second, Anandra insisting as usual that she go through first. Iris appreciated her chivalry, and although she wished that Anandra believed in her ability to take care of herself, it was true that she didn't possess her friend's strength, or her fighting skills, or even her knowledge of this world and its dangers. So Iris didn't object when she was told to go once Anandra decided it was safe.

A few seconds after Anandra went partway through the curtain, she pulled her head back through, reaching for Iris. "You'll want to hold on to me," she told her, and so Iris did, walking through the curtain and almost falling off the edge of a steep cliffside when she got all the way through.

"Fucking hell!" Her legs almost buckled, and she took a few shaky steps back. The curtain was no longer there, a tall, jagged rock wall in its place a mere two or three feet behind where they now stood. "Th...thank you," she said.

Yet again, she owed Anandra a debt for saving her life. No, it really was good that she had her as a guide, because no way could she survive in this strange, magical world, not without Anandra's incredible help. And along with the wonderful rescue she'd just received came an equally wonderful smile, lighting up the moonlit night even brighter than the large white orb that sat full and high in the sky. A dim rainbow circled it, and yet she still preferred Anandra's smile and her beautiful face to the sight of the rainbow-encircled moon that hung above them. She preferred her friend's face by far.

Yep, it was hopeless: she *was* falling for this woman, and a part of her was starting to want to stay here, with her, a part whose wish she would have to deny at the end of their journey.

"What's troubling you, my friend?"

Apparently her face had betrayed her thoughts, and before Iris could stop herself, the truth slipped out. "I was thinking about how I'll have to leave you behind when I go to my home world, and I was thinking about how sad that makes me."

"It makes me sad, too. I've grown to like your company. Very much," Anandra added quickly, and then she coughed into her hand. "Shall we continue? I'd like to find a spot for us to sleep for the night, and I see a good place up ahead, a cave that looks to be just the right size, if my estimations are correct. I hope that when we reach it, you can tell me what you haven't been sharing with me so far. And I do not blame you for not revealing more. I very likely would have done the same."

Iris nodded, and they began to walk toward a cave up ahead. It sat at a wider edge of the path than where they'd quite suddenly landed moments before. When they reached the cave, Anandra told Iris it would do just fine, as it had a small mouth and no other openings inside it, with no way for anyone to sneak up on them without having to go through its only entrance and exit. "Do you really think we have to be that careful now?" Iris watched as Anandra removed a thick blanket from her bag and laid it out on the dirt floor of the cave.

"Of course. It seems that those creatures were after you, and we are very lucky indeed that their attempt at capture—or worse—failed."

Iris didn't like the sound of that "or worse," but she chose to ignore it, instead lying down on the blanket beside Anandra.

As tired as she was, Iris knew she couldn't go to sleep just yet: Anandra had requested that she tell her about everything she'd kept secret up until now. So Iris did, sharing about each of her grandmother's visits and finishing by telling her that apparently she'd lived in that mansion at one point, when she was very young, and so had her grandmother and parents.

"It must have pained you to leave there so soon. I am sorry." Anandra placed her hand over Iris's, giving it a squeeze. The warmth of her palm was comforting, but her gesture and words of support meant more to Iris than she was willing to accept. Why? Why did she have to be falling for her? Why couldn't her relationships be easier? Anandra was clearly a huge leap and a jump above Jane, but this relationship—or whatever it was—couldn't possibly work out.

Iris's eyelids and body weren't the only things that felt heavy as she rolled over and got ready to go to sleep. Her heart was trying to tell her something, something that just couldn't be. But then the comforting heaviness of Anandra's arm landed on top of Iris's waist, and between the warm body behind her and Anandra's slow, steady breath against her neck, she was able to relax and drift off to sleep much sooner than if she'd been all alone.

CHAPTER TEN

The light streaming in through the cave's mouth had almost reached Iris's feet by the time she first opened her eyes. Morning had come, and then some. She was surprised that Anandra had allowed her to sleep in. Her friend was standing by the cave's opening, cutting up some fruit with her knife without looking at her hands. Instead, her eyes were directed toward whatever awaited them outside. "Should I get ready?" Iris asked her, standing up and stretching her arms over her head.

"What?" Anandra's voice sounded far off, and a touch of either sleep or sadness brushed against the edges of it as she said, "Yes, of course. Get ready, and we'll be on our way again. I'll get some food for you, but I'm afraid we don't have time for cheefen. We've got to get going, since I let you sleep in, and I want to keep far ahead of those creatures who attacked your grandmother's home last night."

"Sounds good to me." Iris yawned, then hung her bag over her shoulder. "What about the blanket? Should we get rid of it, so we'll be harder to track?"

"Ah, she's catching on. I'm impressed." Anandra sounded like she was, too. She handed Iris the other two quarters of the large orange fruit, and Iris took her first bite of it gratefully. It was juicy, delicious, and nearly as energizing as the cheefen. Iris almost felt like she didn't need the cheefen, and she wouldn't have killed anyone for a double-shot mocha, either. Was she getting used to this early morning stuff? No, it couldn't be possible.

But she had more than enough energy in her arms and legs to keep up with Anandra without caffeine as Iris happily followed her down the path and in the direction of a long, winding lane, with flowering trees growing on each side of it as far ahead of them as Iris could see.

They reached the lane in what was most likely an hour, although Iris still hadn't taken her watch out of her bag, so it was a loose estimate at best. Another hour or so passed as they walked down the tree-lined path, the occasional breeze tossing the petal-coated branches lightly back and forth, a few pale-white petals ending up in Anandra's hair, to Iris's supreme delight. "You'd look pretty with a wreath from these trees on your head," Iris told her, and Anandra shook her head.

"No, I wouldn't. You surely would, though."

"Yes, you would. It's too bad we don't have the time to stop and make one for each of us."

"We'll be taking a break in a while. Perhaps I will be kind and let you make one for me then."

"That sounds wonderful," Iris told her, and she took Anandra's hand, not caring in the least if it slowed them down. Anandra didn't seem to care either, holding as tight on to her hand as she held on to Anandra's, and Iris had a little spring in her step as she thought about how pleasant it was to be walking through these sweet-smelling trees with a pretty lady's hand in hers. A pretty lady who wasn't Jane, and didn't need to be, for the first time in a year. No, Iris was happy it was Anandra's hand she held.

After passing through what seemed like an almost endless parade of trees and petals, they came to the end of the path. At its end sat a large circle of trees, each of them tall and holding many multicolored flowers. "A pleasure ring. Who would have thought we would be lucky enough to find one here, on our now-different path. I know where we are," Anandra told her, "believe it or not, and I know what we should do next, too." She pulled Iris's hand to her lips and began to suck on Iris's middle finger, her tongue rolling gently against its surface as she sucked away.

Iris had to know. "What is a 'pleasure ring'? Does it cause sexual pleasure?"

Anandra took Iris's finger out of her mouth to answer. "Yes, sexual pleasure. Immense sexual pleasure. When the time and weather are right, as they are now, the petals fall, and they cause lovely sensations on the body as they do, inflicting whatever types of sensations the naked beings beneath them happen to desire."

"Really? Let's try it, then."

Iris let Anandra help her out of her clothes, and then Anandra took off her own. She placed each piece of clothing into an overlapping pile as a makeshift blanket for them to lie upon. As Iris lay down, and Anandra got on top of her, a royal-purple petal managed to find its way in between their lips right as they began to kiss. It made Iris's lips tingle, turning to a sharp, intense sensation after the tingles faded. And then the petal somehow worked its way into Iris's mouth, and she swallowed it, and then the petal's power really began to shine.

She felt it tumbling down her throat while they kissed, caressing it and causing the tingles to turn into slightly stronger vibrations as it slipped deep down inside her. And then a warmth started growing in her stomach, a warmth that slowly turned up its heat, heat that began to make her sweat, each bead of it making her cunt clench and her clit sing with the desire for release as each drop slid down her hot, naked skin.

More petals fell, and still they kissed, and kissed, and each one moaned against the other's lips as the petals brushed against their skin, tumbling against their flesh and finding their way in between them. Iris felt the tender touch of each petal as it reached her skin and felt its touch radiate out across her every surface, spreading until she had to come up for air. "These petals are almost too much," she gasped.

"Then we'll make them too much for me first, and then we'll get you to come while you are overpowered by their magical caress. Put your fingers inside me now, Iris. Put them inside me and make me come."

Iris reached with the arm that had just been wrapped around Anandra's back, sliding it between them and then reaching down farther, until her hand met her partner's mons pubis. She wriggled down a bit until her chin was pressed against Anandra's high upper chest, and it was then that she was finally able to touch her cunt, sliding two fingers between its lips and slipping the tips of them inside. Then she rolled Anandra and herself onto their sides and placed her lips upon one of Anandra's nipples.

This time there wasn't much kink involved, other than Anandra digging her nails into Iris's back as she seemingly became more and more aroused. Iris wanted this to last, though, so she just continued to fuck Anandra's cunt with her fingers, sometimes fast, sometimes slow, not touching her clit for a second, other than letting her hand rub up against it lightly now and then. She sucked on Anandra's nipple while her hand did its duty, enjoying the feel of the soft bud of flesh against her tongue, sucking harder and harder now, as she fucked Anandra, now with three fingers, because Anandra had loosened up quickly, easily allowing the third finger in.

Iris had never fisted a woman before, nor been fisted, but she decided to add it to her to-do list for this trip, and perhaps ask—or beg—Anandra for the honor of her entire hand later. Not to *have* her hand, of course, Iris quickly told herself, and then she returned her focus to Anandra's nipple and cunt, and finally let her fingers get to work on her lover's clit, so round and big and firm by now, so ready to cause Anandra to cry out, to come.

The petals hadn't ceased falling for a second, though, and Iris was still very aware of their presence, their subtle pressure against her skin as each next one fell from its tree and floated down upon her and Anandra. It was then, thinking about the petals, that she had her next brilliant thought. She grabbed a handful of them and pressed them, roughly, against Anandra's pussy, grinding them against it as hard as she could. And with that, Anandra came, unbelievably loudly, and, most likely, unbelievably hard as well.

Iris, like always, got to come next, and Anandra complemented her idea by doing the same thing to her, grabbing a handful of the incredibly soft petals and pushing them hard against Iris's crotch. But instead of grinding them against her, Anandra just held her hand there, strong and stable, cupping her cunt, until Iris couldn't hold off any longer, and she came, too, the pressure and the petals' magic proving to be exactly what she needed to get off. She exploded with a flow of intensity that rushed through her entire body and then seemed to almost pass through her outer being and beyond, possibly going out into the world. She opened her eyes then and saw that the petals around them had frozen in place, levitating midair, and maybe they were waiting for her to stop coming.

When she did—when her orgasm ended—a strong breeze arose and tossed all the petals off them, until a large circle of grass all around them and their clothes was completely free of the petals' many-colored, vibrant rainbow.

"That really did the trick!" Iris said, laughing a little from the joy the petals had caused. And the joy from Anandra's body, too, of course. She couldn't possibly ignore that. She hadn't missed Anandra topping her, even though there had been a few touches of dominance in her actions during this encounter. Just enough to fully sate Iris until they next bedded down together, until their next amazing fuck.

This had almost been more like making love, though, a thought that wouldn't leave Iris alone as she put her clothes back on and combed her fingers through her messy, windswept hair. She was glad she didn't have access to a mirror, because she was guessing it looked frightful, but instead of agreeing with that thought, Anandra told her she liked how messy her hair was. "You look wild, sensual...untamable, too. But I plan on taming you the next time we fuck, or at least trying yet again."

"I'll look forward to your next attempt, in that case." Iris smiled, feeling somewhat shy, but also proud, proud she could do these things to such a fantastic (not to mention incredibly sexy) woman. Yes, she was growing close to Anandra. Too close. Something would have to be done about it, or when she left, she would have to leave all the best parts of herself behind forever. "So," she said, picking up her bag, "do you know where we are?"

❖

A tall woman stroked the long, blond braid falling past her waist as she walked down a dimly lit hallway. She was aware that she was beautiful, sitting in the middle of her prime as looks went. But she also knew, though she preferred not to dwell on it, that something about her looks would never ring entirely true. That was because they were a deception, her blush of youth and beauty coming entirely from magic... magic of the less-welcome, less-kind sort. But it was all she had to help her achieve her goal.

As she walked, she smiled a quiet smile, because she was looking forward to seeing her husband again, after all these years. Or at least she was looking forward to him being of use to her. She was hoping that he would be able to help her with her two current goals and that he would still be able to read the stones. She wanted them to fall in her favor and was almost positive they would. But she had only one way to know—to place the bag she now held in his hands and tell him what she wanted...no, what she *needed* to know.

She reached the door at the end of the hall, pushed it open with a hard, happy shove, and walked into the room. She suppressed a look of disgust as she saw the once-gorgeous man for the first time in over twenty sun-cycles. "My husband!" She gasped. "What has happened? Why have you not kept yourself young?"

The old, wrinkled, balding man in front of her had been smiling when she entered the room, but his lips turned down into a pained grimace upon her words. "Magic is hard to come by when you are exiled as I have been. While you were away, I could barely keep myself fed, having to kill wild animals and eat nasty roots to keep any weight on. You may have been sent to another land, but apparently that land was kinder to you than ours was to me. You are beautiful, though, as you always were. I am sorry you aren't as happy with my looks as I am with yours."

His tone was bitter, and she tried to change her expression back to one of joy at seeing him again, but her mind wouldn't allow it. She wasn't really excited to see him once more, anyway, because his only use in their marriage had been to give her the seat of power and influence she'd once held.

"I have brought the stones for you to read. I am trying once again to rule this world, and I need to be able to best her in order to do that. I want her to bow before me and feel the pain I felt, being exiled for those many sun-cycles, exiled and denied my rightful place on the throne of this land."

"And I am to still rule by your side, am I not?"

"Yes," she lied. "Of course. I would have it no other way. So, are they on their way to the palace? I want your word that you arranged it."

"Yes, yes, she is delivering the letter, and they should reach the palace in two days or less. I see you have something in your hand, though. Is it the stones?"

"Do you still have the ability to read them?"

"Some magic stays with you, even when it's all you have left. I had to trade my own stones for food one cold, horrible winter. It was either that or starve."

"I am sorry to hear that, husband." Another lie, of course, because she was still in need of his help. She had also needed it when she first was able to contact this world again, and she had needed it when it came to returning here. Very little of her connection to her home had remained in the horrible, dark world she'd been sent to. She only hoped the same had happened to her archrival before she had come back to Oria. She had been able to sense the bitch as soon as her feet had first touched the earth here, when she'd come through the portal her husband had made.

It had taken many careful sun-cycles of planning to rebuild her magic stock, to rebuild her army, and now the time was fast approaching when she would put an end to her last threat before conquering this land once and for all. Her magic was not what it used to be, but it would have to do.

"The stones, my dear, if you please," he said.

She handed him the bag and he shook it three times, holding it next to one of his hairy ears as he did so. Yes, it was such a shame that he'd let age take him. He had told her he hadn't had a choice, but she still blamed him for allowing it to happen. She would not have her one roll under the covers with him as planned. No, instead she would provide no treat for her husband before she enslaved him, along with the rest of the lowly idiots of this world.

"Are you ready?"

"Very." She crossed her arms and leered down at him as he opened the bag and dumped out the magical stones. Each was a different color, a different precious stone, and each would display a word, making a sentence that would answer any question from the person asking the stones.

"You've kept your question in mind?" he asked.

"Of course. Tell me, now, what do they say?"

"They say...they say, 'She will lose in the end.'"

"That is exactly what I wanted to hear. Thank you, husband." She leaned down and gave him a kiss on the cheek, doing her best to not flinch as her lips met his leathery skin. Yes, she would have to find a new husband when she took over this land.

Now came the next step in her plan. She only had to wait until they reached the castle, because she knew the young woman would surely be able to do what she, the rightful ruler of this land, was going to trick her into doing. It was her birthright to do so, as her husband had read in the stones all that time ago. And the stones were never, ever wrong.

CHAPTER ELEVEN

Sadly, it was time to leave the magical—and extraordinary—circle of trees after what felt to Iris like far too short a stay. Anandra served her some bread and juice from her bag, eating very little herself. Iris wanted to tell her to have more, because she was almost positive a lot would be asked of Anandra during that day, but she was obviously an adult and could take care of herself well enough without Iris's help.

She couldn't resist asking if Anandra might want to eat a bit more before they left, though.

"I have eaten my fill, really, sweetness, I promise you that. I may not have had my fill of *you*, though!" She grabbed Iris, lifting her off her feet, and spun around in a quick circle. Iris squealed in delight, and Anandra laughed, a high-pitched laugh of complete freedom, one that Iris hadn't heard from her before.

"You have a wonderful laugh," Iris told her once her feet were back on the ground. "You sounded so happy, so glad to be here."

Anandra gave her a pointed stare. "Of course I am, silly. I'm here with you, after all, aren't I?"

Iris had to look away, because the way Anandra was looking at her spoke of more than just lust and sexual needs.

No, it spoke of something far more intense and meaningful than that, and Iris wasn't sure she was ready for Anandra to be looking at her that way, even though, upon gazing back at her, she was pretty much positive that her eyes and smile reflected Anandra's stare and upturned lips. They happened to be lips that she wanted to kiss again, and so she did, still in Anandra's arms, feeling her heat and softness against her own body, wanting to fall to the ground again and make lo…fuck again. Yes, fuck, she thought, not the other thing, because she would have to leave this place. Soon. *Very* soon.

"Should we get going?" She pulled out of Anandra's arms and picked up her bag. "Isn't it time we continued our journey?"

"Yes, I suppose it is. We will be coming to a town soon, I believe, one I haven't been to before, but I have heard from the far-traveled of my home village that they have a wonderful restaurant. I would much rather eat there than dine on my bag's bread, and I'd like to treat you to a good meal, a better one than the last time we dined in public."

"Oh, yes, fewer Neanderthals and shitty drinks would be more than welcome this time. And thank you."

"Neanderthals?"

"They're a version of my species that came many, many years before *Homo sapiens* did, or people like me. Did your species evolve over time, too?"

"Evolve? We became this way, actually, when a mischievous winged creature decided to try to make friends with the sky. It happened ages ago, possibly millions of sun risings and falls. Before my time, in other words."

"You really look like you're closely related to the sky."

"Yes, and my people stand out because of it. In the past, we were said to be able to grant wishes, were you to see a shooting star dance across our skin, but that power seems to have not remained, if it was even there in the first place."

"That's so cool. And you may stand out, but in a good way. I wish my skin was half as beautiful as yours."

"Thank you, then. I must tell you, though: it is. Half as beautiful at the very least!"

Iris laughed. "Onward, then?"

"Yes, indeed, onward."

They gathered up their bags and left the magical circle of trees, and Iris was less than thrilled to leave it behind. It wasn't like she could ever come back here again, after all. She stifled a few sighs as they started down a thin dirt path, winding through knee-high grass and going up and down many small hills. After probably an hour of walking, they reached two towers and a gate, but no sentry or guard blocked their way.

"That was built during the Great War, most likely." Anandra pointed to the gate and the towers, and Iris was relieved to see that she didn't seem angry or devastated at the thought of what had caused her lifelong pain.

Maybe having that cry a while back had helped? Iris hoped it had, because she herself knew what it was like to carry the burden throughout the years of losing those you loved. Now that she could see her grandmother again, her burden had been lessened, but it seemed that Anandra would never be that lucky. Iris made a point to feel her gratitude fully in the moment when they passed through the towers, just as fully as she felt the warm sun once they left the tower's shadows behind.

"I believe the restaurant is down Athet Street, which should be coming up on our left. That's what the most-traveled people of my village said, Lacop and Therie. They've been together many sun-cycles, always adventuring together, and are very much in love. I have to admit, I've felt jealous of them at times." Iris glanced at her face, and when Anandra saw her looking, she quickly added, "I've felt jealous because they've gotten to explore so much, of course. Obviously. Ah, look, Athet Street."

A wooden sign with those words was nailed to a dark-brown pole, and off to their left, on a wide, crowded street, many people were sitting under dark-pink umbrellas at large blue tables, eating and talking and laughing. They were the first people Iris had seen since they entered the town. The area they had entered through seemed to be a part of the town that was much less frequented by the locals. But this restaurant was doing heavy business, by the look of things, and the enticing smells that reached Iris's nostrils as they started down Athet Street quite unsubtly told her why.

A combination of foreign spices and herbs had delighted her nostrils by the time they reached the restaurant. She and Anandra walked through its wide-open front door. This place seemed a lot friendlier than their last restaurant experience, with people and creatures of many different ages and types inside, all the races and creatures mixed together at each of the tables and booths.

At least, it seemed friendly until the people and creatures began to notice them, and then a hush fell over the room. Did they really stand out that much? Iris felt almost as uncomfortable as she'd felt at the place in Rivest, even though these folks seemed far less scary and creepy than the men who had filled the room there.

Just as abruptly as the talking had stopped and the staring had started, it changed back, the people and magic beings turning back to their food. A short man with whiskers and orange, cat-like ears, as well as a striped orange-and-black tail, walked over to them, holding what must have been menus in his left hand. "Would you like a table for two?" he asked them. Or at least he asked one of them, his pale-yellow eyes with black, slitted pupils not leaving Iris's face for a second.

"Yes, for two. Thank you." Iris would have stared just as intensely at him if she hadn't become rather used to the immense variety of beings and people in this world by now. Could he tell she wasn't from this world? Was that why everyone there had stopped mid-bite and stared at them? But Iris couldn't do anything about the staring, and besides, they had arrived at their table while she'd been mulling this over, and so she decided to turn her own attention to the restaurant's wonderful scents and the view of a colorful garden right outside the window they were seated next to. A small bunch of flowers in a vase sat on their table, most likely from a bush of purple-fading-to-pink blooms she could see growing a few feet beyond the window.

"Would you like drinks to start?"

"Do you have any ciders you'd recommend?" Anandra turned to Iris and winked.

"We have a local one, made from the freshest fruit you can imagine. One or two?"

"Do you want to give our ciders another chance?"

"I guess I will, but only because you're paying."

Anandra laughed at that. "Two, sir—two ciders."

A few minutes later, two mugs full of red, fizzing liquid arrived. Iris took a tentative sip, ready to be disgusted again. "Wow, that's really good."

"Why thank you, miss," their waiter said. "That means a lot coming from you."

"Coming from *me*? What do you mean?"

"Oh, nothing," he answered quickly. "Nothing at all. What'll you be having, then?"

Anandra looked down at the menu, then back up at Iris. "May I order for you?"

"Sure, I'd prefer it if you did."

"Two vren sandwiches and some chopped potatoes. Do those come with the usual dipping sauce?"

"Only the finest sauce in the village, if I do say so myself."

"That sounds great, then."

"I'll be back with your order. And your food is on us today, miss." Another sharp look came with his words. What was up with him? He was practically treating them like royalty, and Iris didn't have any idea why.

"What's with our waiter?" she asked Anandra, keeping her voice as low as she could as she leaned across the table.

"I have no guesses, but we should eat quickly and then go. And I will insist upon paying for our food. I do not want any favors when I don't know why I'm receiving them." Anandra's eyes weren't on Iris when she spoke. Instead, she had turned her head slightly away from Iris and appeared to be scanning what she could of the room. "I don't know what's going on, but I hope it's nothing bad."

"Me, too, Anandra, me, too."

Their food arrived only moments later. Iris had no idea how they'd managed to make what looked to be two meat sandwiches and oven-baked fries so fast. Maybe...yeah, they'd probably gotten special treatment based on whatever the kitchen and their waiter thought was true about her and Anandra. Or just her, actually, because it was becoming clear to Iris that it wasn't her friend who was getting everyone all worked up in a tizzy. She dug into her food, which turned out to be just as delectable as Anandra's friends had said. But instead of lingering over each bite of the delicious sandwich, fries, and rich, creamy dipping sauce, she wound up eating as fast as she could, and then, her plate mostly empty, she made eye contact with Anandra.

"You ready?"

"Yes. But let me convince them to let us pay, first."

The waiter seemed to have noticed they were getting ready to leave, rushing back to their table with a small plate covered in what looked like various types of fruit desserts. "This dessert was your mother's favorite whenever she'd eat with us. I hope you like it as well as she did."

"My mother? Who do you think I am, anyway?"

"Why, Selehn's granddaughter. You have her eyes and mouth, maybe other things as well. You must be her daughter's child."

The name Selehn sounded rather familiar to Iris, but before she could ask him who this Selehn person was, Anandra rose from the table and threw some coins onto it. "I hope that's enough for lunch. Iris, time to leave. Let's go." She pulled Iris up and eased her in the direction of the door. Iris was only able to look back for a few seconds, seeing a look of supreme disappointment on the waiter's face.

He held up his hand during those few seconds, waving at her like she was an old friend. "Thank you for coming, miss! Please do come back—we'd love to serve you again! Any time, day or night!"

"Now what was that all about?" Iris asked once they were outside again. The waiter's personal treatment had made her incredibly curious about who Selehn was and why she'd meant so much to this man, and now it was too late to ask him for any more information. "And why were you in such a rush to leave?"

"I…I don't know. I just felt compelled to get out of there.

The waiter's actions were too unpredictable, as were the actions of the ones lunching there. And no way could you be Selehn's granddaughter. That would just be too…too impossible."

"Who was this Selehn person, again? Her name sounds very familiar to me, for some reason."

"I'd rather not speak of her. She may have saved the land, but she wasn't able to stop my parents from being killed. We should leave this town and quickly get back on the road, because I think if we keep on our way, we can reach the castle by sometime tomorrow."

"That sounds good to me." Iris wasn't sure if she meant those words, but she wasn't really fully present at the moment, anyway. She also wasn't really paying attention to whatever it was Anandra said when she started telling Iris some kind of history of this city, learned from the friends who had visited here. No, she was mostly tuning out Anandra's words, instead focused almost completely on what had happened in the restaurant.

She was still thinking about it when they reached the edge of the town a while later, but the appearance of a wide, fast-moving river up ahead brought her back to reality. "How are we going to get across that?" she asked Anandra. "I'm not that good of a swimmer."

"*I* am good enough at swimming to cross it, but look farther upstream. There's a Boat Sender and his raft a number of steps up from where we stand." Anandra pointed, and now Iris saw a wooden raft up ahead, floating on their side of the river. Some sort of large bug seemed to be flying around above it, buzzing up a few inches and then down a few, a very strangely shaped bug.

"Is it safe?" she asked, following Anandra in the raft's direction. As Iris had told her, she really couldn't swim very well. In fact, if she fell into this deep-looking, fast-flowing water, she probably wouldn't make it back out without a ton of magic. And a miracle—or two—would probably be required alongside the magic.

"The Boat Senders are experts, Iris. You have absolutely nothing to worry about."

"That's what my grandmother told me the first time I tried to learn to swim, actually. It isn't really what I needed to hear."

"Sorry." Anandra sounded only slightly remorseful, but Iris decided that would have to do. And so would the Boat Sender and the raft, she decided, giving it a wary once-over as they arrived at its docking point.

A very small winged creature fluttered above the rope attaching the raft to the shore, wearing a brown cloth shirt and matching pants. He had wings that seemed decidedly fairy-like to Iris, blue and gold and slightly translucent, shimmering in the sun in a most captivating way. She easily could have stayed on shore and stared at his wings for an hour or two, instead of getting on the un-water-worthy-looking boards, bound together with thin, black rope and with very slight spaces in between their lengths. Now *that* looked like it could sink any moment, Iris thought with what she hoped was an imperceptible shudder.

"Are you all right?" Anandra asked. Imperceptible? Apparently not.

"I'll be okay. Just promise me you won't hesitate to give me mouth-to-mouth. After all, it worked pretty well the first time."

"I'd rather give you mouth-to-mouth in private," Anandra said softly, words that caused Iris to grin.

"What are you talking about, ladies?" the fairy-like creature asked. "Is it funny? It looks like it's funny. I love good jokes, but I'm bad at telling them. Ask any of my friends."

"That was funny, actually," Anandra told him. "Now, what do you charge to take people across this river?"

"It was? It really was? I was trying to be funny, actually," he said, but his words didn't sound all that believable to Iris. He seemed sweet, though, and rather innocent as well. Hopefully he was as good at ferrying as he was bad at lying.

"Can you get us across safely?" Iris asked, scanning the water as it rushed past the land where she stood.

"Yes, ma'am! I'm the best of the winged folk at ferrying. Everyone says that. I may not be funny, but I'm good at my job. And I only charge one gray coin per customer, too!" He sounded quite proud of all of this, and Iris hoped his pride was very, *very* justified.

"That's quite the deal, little one," Anandra told him. "The last winged woman who ferried me across a river charged two yellow coins and some bread. How about I throw in some fruit? Or cheefen?"

"Oh, no cheefen for me! I had it once and couldn't sleep for three days! I have plenty of energy anyway, ask anyone!"

It sounded like he enjoyed being asked about, Iris thought. Either that or he was uncertain about what was true about him and what wasn't. Iris hoped his statement about his skill at ferrying was true, at the very least, and so with a small gulp, she boarded the raft and sat as close to its very center as she could. Anandra boarded next, sitting beside her, and she handed the winged creature a small silver coin from her sack and a small, pink berry.

"Have any of those left?" Iris asked. Maybe eating on the way across would help to distract her.

"Here." Anandra handed her three of the pink berries, and as the winged creature untied the rope and held out his arm in the direction of the other side, Iris popped all three berries into her mouth and began to chew. She had barely swallowed her small mouthful when the raft slowly floated upward and began to move across the river—about three feet above the water! Iris didn't know if it made her more scared or less, but she realized that it meant Anandra might be able to catch her before she hit the water's surface.

"So," Iris asked the little guy, hoping he could distract her with some talking, "what's your name?"

"My name? It's Lutho, Lutho Bon Cari Wihld Shine. But you can call me Lutho. What's yours? And yours?"

Iris was relieved that he didn't look at either of them while he introduced himself. If it were up to her, he wouldn't look away from the other side of the river for even a millisecond. "My name is Iris, and this is Anandra. It's nice to meet you, Lutho."

"You, too. Well, since I'm guessing you two ladies aren't from around here, I should tell you something. It's not good, by the way. Not good at all."

Lutho sounded like he was positive these particular words were true, and Iris didn't like that one bit. "What is it, then? Please, tell us."

"There's word among my people that trouble is coming to our land. Or, actually, trouble is already here. The word is also that someone has returned from a far-away place. No one knows who yet, but they know it isn't good, not good at all. The person or being or whatever they are…well, they're very evil. My people can sense such things. I'm only still working because I need the money to help a sick friend, or I would have left by now. Anyway, we're all worried that it might have to do with what happened twenty-and-some sun-cycles ago. Some of my people have heard about the clay warriors being back, but that couldn't possibly be true."

"No, it is." Anandra sounded none too pleased telling him this, and a look of fear rushed across Lutho's petite features.

"Really?! No! No, not good, not good!"

The raft shook a little and tilted slightly to the left. Iris shrieked and grabbed onto Anandra, but then the raft righted itself. But the next thing that happened to the raft seemed almost worse to Iris, at least when it came to her fear of drowning—the raft began to speed up, faster and faster, until it was positively rushing toward the other side of the river. Lutho and the raft were shaking equally, equally *greatly*, which didn't exactly help Iris feel any safer.

"Lutho, calm yourself. I will help you, I promise, but you *must* get us safely to the other side." Anandra sounded more in control than either Lutho seemed or Iris felt, and her steady voice calmed Iris enough to remind herself to take a deep breath and try to calm down, too. Lutho seemed to have the same idea, Anandra's voice and words having the desired effect, and moments later the raft slowly drifted down to the shore on the other side of the river, landing on the ground instead of on the water.

"Phew!" Lutho wiped his brow with one of his tiny hands and slowly flew down to the ground, landing on what looked like very shaky legs. Iris's weren't much more stable than his, but she managed to get to her feet when Anandra offered Iris her hands, letting her pull her up onto the dry land, which she was quite grateful to have back beneath her feet.

"Lutho, I have something for you." Anandra reached into her bag and held out a handful of shiny gold coins. "Will this be enough to help your friend and to allow you to leave the land?"

"Oh, my, oh, my, oh, my! Yes, yes, it will. Thank you, Anandra! Thank you, Iris! I will never, ever forget this." Lutho held out his arms, and Anandra placed the coins into his trembling hands one by one, giving him four gold coins in total.

"You're very welcome, Lutho. I like helping kind people, and you've given us some very useful information."

"I hoped it would be. Good-bye, now, ladies, and good luck. Much, much good luck." Lutho nodded at Iris and Anandra and then flew off.

"That was incredibly sweet of you, you know," Iris told Anandra, and she leaned forward and gave her a small kiss on the cheek.

"He seemed like a dear little fellow to me, a truly good example of a man and a friend. I hope his sick friend actually exists," she added in a gruff voice, but Iris guessed she was just trying to sound tough. She knew Anandra well enough by now that Iris was positive she was also a truly good example of a woman and a friend. And a truly good example of a lover, too.

They set off down a path through some thinly scattered trees. Iris might have been grateful to get safely across the river, but she was more grateful to be staring at Anandra's lovely ass and curves. The woman in front of her had become someone Iris was growing to care about deeply, despite her best efforts. But she tried to concentrate on her friend's body and nothing else, as Anandra led her in what Iris hoped was the direction of a bed and some privacy: so she could experience those curves and that ass in more detail, and so she could spend some time, one-on-one, with Anandra. She found herself thinking, then, that she had grown to care for Anandra much more than she was comfortable with, and much more than would allow her to travel home without emotional pain.

This sucks, she thought as she followed Anandra through the woods. *This really, really sucks.*

CHAPTER TWELVE

Iris had heard of the giant iguanas of the Galapagos Islands, but she'd never seen any of them walking upright, nor had she seen any of them dressed in long tunics of varied colors, tunics that seemed to be made of shimmery fabric like silk or satin. And admittedly, these amphibians in front of her and Anandra didn't look like iguanas. They looked more like the blue-bellied salamanders she'd caught when she'd gone to her family's regular vacation spot each year. She'd always been very careful not to hurt them when she'd caught them, and so she hoped these much-larger versions that she and Anandra had just met up with were just as peaceful and non-nipping. The salamanders at the cabin by the river had never so much as gummed her while she'd held them.

"Hello?" she said, more of a question than a greeting.

Just seconds ago, the salamanders had somewhat suddenly appeared on the path she and Anandra were on. They'd come from a clearing in the trees to the left and seemed to be headed off to the right. In that direction, the trees thinned out, blocking the mid-afternoon sun only now and then, but slow-moving pale-pink clouds had given her and Anandra enough shade to fully block the sun's heat. It had been a very hot day around noon, and the trees around them then were much more sparse. Iris noticed now that her sweating had only recently started to slow. She'd hoped Anandra wouldn't mind her strengthened scent, but Anandra's nose hadn't wrinkled while she'd walked close at her side, so at the very least it hadn't bothered her.

"Greetings," replied the salamander who stood slightly in front of the rest—there were about ten or twelve of them, all dressed in the same long, flowing, and quite pleasing-to-the-eye tunics, clearly finely made. The salamander who had spoken was also wearing what looked like a fez, red to match his clothing, and it had a thin, black tassel hanging from its top. The tassel's tip bounced slightly when he spoke, but Iris only barely noticed its merry little dance, because he was her first talking salamander, and he was also almost her size. Based on their physical size, and also the size of their group, these beings might prove to be a threat.

"Greetings," said a few of the other salamanders, in low, soothing voices, and the one in the front bowed slightly. *That* didn't seem threatening! Iris thought.

"It is such a delight to run across one of your kind," the salamander in the fez said, turning toward Anandra. "Two of your people saved my father's life in the Great War, and I am forever grateful to them. I believe their names were…Sena and Rhan. Yes, they camped with him and me for a few days, telling us stories of their daughter back at home. They loved her dearly, they told me. I don't suppose…"

Anandra's eyes were wet, and she rubbed at them roughly with her left hand. "No," she said in a scratchy voice. "No, they weren't my parents, but I knew them, and they were dear to me, almost like another mother and father, we were so close. Thank you, hathlal. Now I must incline my head and body to you, for you have brought me a great gift." Anandra bowed slightly at the waist for a few seconds, then rose with both a smile and a few tears upon her face.

"They were very brave, you should know. They saved

many lives in our camp beyond just my father's. They even saved mine. Sena shielded me when one of the clay warriors shot an arrow at me, and it only barely missed her heart. I don't think…did they…?"

"No, they didn't make it home to us," Anandra answered.

"Here." Iris held out her arms before she could consider that Anandra might not want her to. "Come and get a hug, sweetie." She was surprised at her own use of a pet name, but she was more surprised when Anandra gladly took her up on her offer, falling into her arms and holding her incredibly tight to her breast. A few of the salamanders (or hathlal) placed their hands on them, making soft clicking and humming noises that sounded quite compassionate to Iris. Apparently they weren't a threat in the least, unless it was to Anandra's ability to stay stoic.

After a shockingly long hug, Anandra slowly moved away from her, placing her now-free arm around the hat-wearing salamander. "Please," she said, turning her head slightly down and looking into his eyes. "Please, join us in a small meal from my bag and tell me anything you can of my family friends. I never saw them again after the war began, and I am desperate to hear anything at all you can tell me or remember about them."

"I am more than happy to do so, my new friend," he answered, and Anandra led the troop of hathlal to a small circle of rocks slightly off the path to their left.

As they ate some fruit and bread from Anandra's bag, the hat-wearing leader of the group introduced himself as Kee and told her all he could recall of the time he spent living with her close friends. He told her about how they always shared any food more than generously, sometimes going hungry just so children they met on their travels could eat. He told her of the many lives they had saved, and how, after a while, they had left, going off in the direction of the castle to hopefully meet up with Selehn and help her overthrow the evil Queen, giving Iris the chance to remember where she'd heard her possible grandmother's name. But she couldn't possibly interrupt, not when this meant so much to Anandra. The salamander finished by saying that he didn't know if her friends had ever reached Selehn, but he did hear that they had fought in a great battle, yet again showing their heroic nature.

Neither Iris's nor Anandra's eyes were dry by the end of his tale, and some of the hathlal were tearing up as well, making quiet gulping noises every now and again.

"That is all I know," Kee said finally. "But have you heard the news? There is word that the Sreth—or the ex-queen, as you may call her—has returned, and so you two should keep off the main road as much as you can. Heed my words, brave women, heed them and keep safe. Shortly before dark, you should reach an inn about three sun-falls up the path. When you come upon it, knock three times, and the innkeeper will let you in. He serves very delicious worms."

Iris couldn't help making a face of disgust as the idea of dining on worms crossed her mind. "He serves good people food, too," Kee added with a chuckle. "Please take care, and remember," he said, rising to his hind legs, "keep off the path, and go nowhere near the castle."

"We will," Anandra told him, smiling and bowing again, but Iris knew it was a lie. Then Anandra also rose, and Iris followed her and the hathlal back to the path. They continued on their way, starting at the right of her and Anandra, and Kee bowed again as they walked away, seeming to smile as he made eye contact with Anandra. As he and his fellow travelers marched off into the woods, Anandra surprised Iris yet again, taking her hand and giving it a tight squeeze.

"I cannot begin to tell you how much our meeting with the hathlal meant to me," she said in a still slightly teary voice.

"You don't have to," Iris told her. "I can easily imagine how you felt." She turned to Anandra and smiled widely. "Should we continue on our way, then?"

"Yes, yes. I hope this inn they spoke of really does serve something other than worms," Anandra joked. "I only like my long, skinny food to have never lived, and to be coated in a good, rich sauce."

"That sounds like the pasta of my world," Iris said, following Anandra back onto the path and back in the direction they'd been headed. She wasn't all that happy to have heard the hathlal's warning about going to the castle, but she hoped he was wrong. After all, everything they'd heard so far hadn't necessarily indicated that the castle would be unsafe, unless this being who had returned to the land wanted to overthrow the current Queen. Wouldn't that be great, if they were to arrive at the castle, all ready to send Iris home, and instead got ambushed? Wouldn't that be great, indeed.

Just as the salamanders had said, they arrived at a place to stay the night about two hours later, by Iris's guess. However, their place to stay the night happened to be a large, flat rock. Wide enough to sleep on, but in no way was it an inn, especially one that served delicious worms, unless they were crawling around its bottom edges.

"This is where it should be, for I see nothing for miles ahead except for the castle." As Anandra said this, Iris turned slightly to her left and saw turrets and everything: not too far in the distance, probably no more than a day's walk, stood a white castle, sitting on a slight rise on the otherwise flat path leading in its direction.

"We're almost there!" Excitement rose inside Iris. She

was almost home. But…was that what she really wanted? Did she really want to go home?

Anandra seemed not to have heard Iris speak, pacing the area around the rock. "I wonder if it's hollow," she mumbled, and she knocked on it twice.

"You might as well knock on it a third time," Iris told her.

She had been joking, but Anandra did just as she'd suggested, and suddenly, a large brick building with two stories and two round windows on either side of an open door appeared right in front of them. Iris jumped at its sudden appearance, but Anandra looked pleased instead of startled. "May we enter?" she asked the short, balding man who stood in its open doorway. "I have coin, of course."

"Please do," the man said, opening the door a little wider. Then, "Please do!" he shouted. "Please do, and hurry—danger is almost upon us!"

Anandra pushed Iris inside, following right after her, and the innkeeper shut and locked the door behind them. He reached into a giant pot by the front door and tossed some blue powder onto the door, murmuring some words in an unfamiliar tongue.

"Are we cloaked once more?" Anandra asked him.

He turned to them, glancing from face to face with wide eyes. "Yes, yes. Let's go to the window and watch. I want to make sure they don't try to enter."

They all crowded around one of the inn's large round windows. Coming down the path, in the direction of the castle, were three of the creepy clay warriors they'd seen a few days ago. One of them held a chain, and a snarling, gray, three-headed hound yanked on it, clearly wanting to get free. As the three warriors and the hound drew closer to the rock, the hound's heads all turned in the direction of the inn. Each of its noses began to sniff furiously, and one head tilted toward the sky and howled, the other two heads growling as it pulled the warrior straight toward the building where Iris, Anandra, and the innkeeper hid.

Iris gasped and placed a hand in front of her open lips, more scared than she had been at any point since their trip had begun. She hoped the beast wouldn't be able to enter the inn, and she hoped that if it could, it wouldn't be as hungry as its three drooling mouths seemed to imply. It drew closer and closer to the window they stood behind, scenting the air as steam rushed out of its nostrils. Then, the warrior yanked it roughly back and kicked its side with a loud *thump*. "There's nothing there, you stupid, worthless sack of shit."

The dog whimpered, and Iris found herself feeling sorry for it. Her compassion wasn't the only thing on her mind, though, because a small black circle was now floating midair near their front door, and it was quickly getting bigger. Soon it was twice as wide as the inn's front door, and Iris could see a woman inside it, her blond hair pulled away from her face. She was quite beautiful, although she was also rather hard looking. Iris felt an instant mistrust of this woman, mistrust that was apparently justified, as the woman turned to the warriors, pointing at them with a look of anger and disappointment painted across her pretty features.

She didn't appear attractive anymore when she began to yell at the warriors, her elegant face now twisted into a look of fury and hate. "Get the fuck in here! He was wrong!" She huffed out an angry breath. "Besides," she muttered, a sharp grin spreading across her lips, "we'll get what we want soon enough. No reason to rush things when they're obviously going to go according to plan. Yes, get in here, you idiots. Hurry up!" She turned and stomped off, probably to yell at someone else, and the warriors and their hound quickly entered the portal, following her down a hallway just a few steps as the portal shrank to nothing, and then the warriors and the woman were gone.

"Oh, my!" Iris heard from behind her, and she watched as Anandra only barely managed to catch the innkeeper as his eyes rolled back and he fainted.

Anandra turned to Iris. "Help me get the poor man into that chair in front of the fireplace. It seems he's suffered quite a shock, and I want to see if my bag can provide something to bring him back to consciousness, so that we may question him and see if he will tell us why that woman scared him so."

"Yes, and let's do it for his health, too."

"Of course." Anandra slung one of his arms over her shoulder, and Iris took the other, dragging him over to a tall-backed, leather armchair that sat directly in front of an unlit stone fireplace. They lowered him into the chair, and Iris sat down on a matching leather sofa to the chair's right, checking his pale, round face for signs of life as Anandra rustled around in her bag. After a few moments, she said, "Aha!" and pulled out a small, stoppered vial.

She uncorked it and waved it under his nose, and he came to with a loud gasp, and then followed the gasp with the shouted words, "Oh no...Oh no! She has returned! Tressa has returned! And with no Selehn here to save us, we are clearly doomed!"

Chapter Thirteen

A nandra took a large step back and appeared to almost drop the vial she'd used to revive the innkeeper. "How do you know?" she asked him, her voice full of wariness.

"I know because Selehn lived here for not nearly enough sun-cycles, with her partner, Brenne."

Now it was Iris's turn to take a step back in shock. This was far too much of a coincidence. This man had known her grandmother? "Selehn? Do you mean Sallie? My grandma?"

But the innkeeper, who was still a little dazed from his fainting spell, continued without answering Iris's question. "And her daughter, Ria, had fallen in love with my son, Harthane, a while before they moved here. They had a daughter, Iris, and then…then everything went wrong when Tressa hunted Selehn down, after she'd lost the war and been sent into hiding. Brenne and Selehn and even Ria did most of the planning for winning the war, but I was able to contribute my own magical skills. I'd always had a pretty good hand when it came to magic, and I taught Selehn everything I knew. And then some! Boy, was she a quick learner. Surpassed me in under half a sun-cycle, I should say. If only…if only I hadn't… well, ladies, how about I feed you two a meal and tell you the whole tale?"

"You still didn't answer my question, and I'd really like to know if we're talking about the same person." Iris was never this rude, but she felt if any situation allowed for rudeness, this one truly did. After all, this man might be her grandfather! "By the way," she said, bending down and extending her hand, "my name's Iris. Nice to meet you."

"Oh, dear, Iris! It couldn't be! But you do look more than a little like her, like Ria. The eyes, and the nose, yes, and the hair a fair bit, too. Well, I will bring out my best alcohol, in that case. And may I…I mean, if you are her…may I be allowed to hug my granddaughter?"

"Yes," Iris said, feeling all choked up. "Yes, you definitely may."

"Wonderful, my dear. Oh, this is wonderful." The elderly man slowly rose from his chair, reached out his arms, and enveloped Iris in a gentle hug. He held her for a long time, but Iris didn't care. She certainly wouldn't complain about meeting her paternal grandfather for the first time, nor would she complain about him hugging her.

"Now then, what do you ladies like to eat? And where did you wind up, when I screwed up so horribly and sent you away from this land?"

"*You* sent me away? Is that how I left this land and wound up on Earth?"

"Earth, ah, so that's where you landed. Is it different from here? Is the magic as strong there?" He gestured toward a door to the left of the fireplace. "Kitchen's this way. I always prefer to eat in there with my close friends when they visit. I could make my secret stew, if you'd like. Or roast scuene. I have a good one hanging in my larder. Could use some herbs and the last touch of my magic meat sauce I have left. Yes, I think this occasion calls for it. By the way, my name's Kahar. I was named after my father's father."

He went through the door he'd gestured toward, and they followed him through it. Iris was still trying to wrap her head around things. She'd just met her grandfather for the first time. And he'd known her grandmother, Sallie, and her partner, Brenne. And his son was her father, whom, just like her mother, she'd barely met in her childhood. Did he possibly have photos of them? Wait, did photos even exist in this world?

She was far too full of questions, but she decided she'd hold them back while her grandfather cooked dinner and told them the rest of whatever story he wanted to tell them.

In the kitchen, he pushed through two waist-height swinging doors on the far wall and came out carrying a small pig-like creature, which apparently had been skinned, and a bowl with some fresh green leaves in a bundle, along with something that looked like an orange, and a small blue bottle with a cork in it. He placed the bowl on a marble-topped island and then plopped the pig creature onto a block of wood. Then he pointed to some stools on the far side of the island.

"Go ahead and sit down. The scuene will take at least ten minutes for the magic sauce to kick in, and I'll still have to rub it with the herbs and maconifruit. Besides, I want to explain what you must be wondering about—how you ended up separated from your mother and father, sent from this world and into a completely different realm. I hate to have to tell you this, but it was all my fault, all just a slight slip of my tongue and the magic then went completely wrong."

"I'm sure it was an accident," Iris said, smiling at him as gently and kindly as she could. Poor guy, still feeling guilty about a mistake he'd made her entire lifetime ago. Still, if *she* had done something like that, even if twenty years of her adult life had passed since her mistake, she'd probably still be beating herself up as well. Especially if it had to do with family.

"Whether it was an accident or not—which it was, of course—it still keeps me up nights. I haven't slept well since I sent my entire remaining family away. And all just to get rid of Tressa. Here, I'll get started preparing the meal and tell you while I cook. I promise you, I know my way around meat. You won't be disappointed."

As he prepared the scuene and began to cook some root vegetables in a large skillet, he turned back to them from time to time, and the whole time he was cooking, he explained what had happened that caused Iris, her parents, her grandmother, and Brenne to be sent from Oria.

Apparently, her grandmother had plotted out most of her moves from this very inn during the war, using Kahar's teachings to travel via portal to wherever her powers were needed most. The people and creatures of the land had stood by her with immense loyalty, many of them dying in order for the war to be won, and those who died were always proud to give their lives to the cause, to protect their families and friends back at home.

But then things had taken a turn for the worse: word came that Queen Tressa had discovered where Selehn and her family were hiding out, and so Brenne, Selehn, and Kahar had hatched a quick and desperate plan. They hadn't told anyone else because the magic they planned to use to attempt to stop Tressa was closer to the dark side of things and would take great power to use, so much that the person using this particular spell ran the risk of not surviving the casting of it.

Because of the inherent risk in using this spell, Kahar had hatched his own plan. When Tressa had appeared outside the inn, and when she'd broken through its protective magics, Kahar had cast the spell himself, before Selehn had the chance to. But instead of sending only Tressa to another world, Kahar's family was split up and magicked away as well. Iris had been in Brenne's arms, and so she was sent to Earth with Brenne and Selehn, who had been touching her partner. Kahar had no idea where Iris's parents had gone. Nor did he know where Tressa had ended up, although he knew enough to realize that she'd at least gone to a different place than his and Iris's family.

"But oh! To have been separated from my son, my daughter-in-law, my grandchild. And Brenne, and Selehn, whom I had grown so close to as well. And for you to be separated from your parents. I just can't forgive myself, I just can't."

"You must, Kahar—I want you to!" Iris got up from her stool and went over to Kahar, placing her hands on his upper arms. She squeezed them, looking up into his teary eyes as she said, "I forgive you, if that helps."

"It does, Granddaughter, it really does. How is Selehn, though? And Brenne? And how the heck did you wind up back here?"

"I think something drew me back here, something important, but I haven't yet discovered what it was. And Selehn, Sallie, she's here, too. Brenne died when I was still very young, and Sallie disappeared when I was young, too. I think that somehow she got magically pulled back into this world, although I still don't know why, or how. It turned out that Brenne couldn't survive in a world without magic, though, and maybe that was what brought Sallie back here, too. It seems the people from here need magic to live."

Iris leaned up against the counter next to the stove as Kahar stirred the vegetables in the pan. They were browning nicely, and she could smell the herbed, citrusy scent of the scuene's dressing, as well as the richness of its meat. She had no doubt that dinner would be as delicious as Kahar had promised. But she still had questions before she could let herself eat, including one especially important one. So she took in a breath. "I have to know something."

"Of course, dear, of course. Ask me anything."

"Do you know what Tressa is planning? Why she's back? And do you think that I'm right in guessing that it involves me somehow?"

"I couldn't say what she's planning, not at all, but I wish I could tell you you're wrong, say that it won't require you in some way or another. My advice to you is…well, to be honest, I don't know how it could be possible, but Anandra must know better than me. Because I was pretty sure I had the last of the power required to send people from this world to other ones. Are you positive this will be possible, young lady?"

"Uh, not entirely positive, but it's her best bet." Now that was new! Iris had thought up until those words that Anandra could get her home, without a doubt.

"My best bet?" She turned to Anandra, feeling slightly wary of her for the first time in a while.

"I'm almost positive my tutor can help you. He's done it before. He told me when I was his student. Yes, he's done it, at the very least once." Anandra took a swallow of her drink and smiled at Iris, who couldn't help but smile back. No way Anandra was misleading her. No way.

"And I promise we'll find another path if he can't do it. You have my word."

And you have my heart. The thought came out of nowhere. Iris looked at Anandra then, to try to see what her face was saying right then, but she was gazing out the kitchen's window now, and Iris couldn't see her face at all.

"I'm hoping he can do it, then." Kahar nodded twice at Iris, bringing her attention back to him and away from whatever her crazy little heart might be thinking. "I hope so. Because your world is where you'll be safe, and you should just let us magic folk take care of ourselves. I want you away from Tressa's grasp, far away from it, because it seems that whatever she has planned, it involves you in some way."

"Maybe." Iris went back over to where Anandra sat.

Iris glanced at her, and she now had a noticeable stiffness to her body and face, a stiffness that also was in her voice when she said, "I agree with Kahar. You need to be kept safe. I insist upon it." She turned to Iris and cupped her cheek. "We just can't have anything bad happen to you. I will make it my duty to keep you safe from here on out. It's a shame that the only way to get you home lies at the castle. I wish I knew what might await us there, but there's only one way to find out."

"Yeah, only one way." Iris wasn't really listening to Anandra's words right then, though; she was listening to her feelings instead, feelings that were pulling her between the thought of staying with Anandra forever and her interest in self-preservation. She knew she belonged on Earth, or at least she thought she knew. Maybe she'd have a better idea about all this in the morning, after a good night's sleep and, first, a good meal (and hopefully some better-than-good sex afterward).

Iris had been right: the meal was delicious, and her grandfather's finest alcohol, which was very similar to an excellent merlot, was more than deserving of being called his finest. Her grandfather told her all about her parents as they ate, and she barely noticed how quiet Anandra was throughout the meal, her attention completely on Kahar as she heard about the parents she couldn't remember.

"It is so wonderful that you are able to speak to Selehn, to Sallie, as you call her, once more. I hope you will have a chance for a reunion, but in case you have a reunion with another, much less likeable member of our world, let me give you something to help you." Kahar left the kitchen and came back holding a small, squat white object that turned out to be a thick candle. "I don't know what it will do, believe it or not, just that it was my grandfather's prized magical possession, and it is supposed to stop evil in its very tracks—and then some. But the problem is that its other necessary part, its magical lighting match, was lost many sun-cycles ago, so I don't know how much use the candle will be without it."

Kahar glanced around the room as if looking for something, and then his eyes settled on a spot near the stove. "Here, perhaps these will do the trick." He picked up a small box of matches from the counter next to the stove and handed them to Iris.

"Thank you, Kahar. Thank you very much."

"Yes, Kahar, many thanks." Anandra inclined her head to him in a slight bow, and he bowed back at her. "But now we must turn in for the night, because we still have some traveling left tomorrow, and based on the monsters' and Tressa's return, I want to have as much energy as possible come morning for whatever may come to pass."

"That sounds very smart, Anandra. Let me lead you to your quarters, then. I will of course be giving you my finest room, and I hope it's obvious that you will not be charged." His cheeks dimpled up as he grinned.

Kahar led them up some stairs to the left of the main room's fireplace, through a wooden door and into a large flowery bedroom. A king-sized bed sat in its middle, with a love seat, a round blue coffee table, and two chairs to the bed's left. Upon looking up, Iris was impressed to see a candle-filled chandelier, which filled the room with a soft golden glow. "Sleep well, you two, and don't hesitate to wake me if you need anything. You are family, after all. Oh, and Iris?"

"Yes, Kahar?"

"Was I correct in assuming you wouldn't need separate rooms?"

Iris's face grew hot, and she averted his eyes. "Um, yeah."

"You'll hear no judgments from me, not a single one. I'm just glad you've found someone."

Me, too, Iris thought as Kahar left. But she'd found someone who, sadly, would not be in her life for much longer. Iris decided to make the best of her last night with Anandra, a night that seemed like it might have come too soon. Hopefully, the candles wouldn't be the only thing lighting up the room tonight. Hopefully, some sun-bright fireworks would explode when she and Anandra began kissing.

Which was now the case, only moments after they'd been left alone, Anandra's lips soft on hers. Her tongue felt even softer as it licked at Iris's bottom lip and then slid into her mouth. It was more than welcome to do so, and Anandra's hands were welcome wherever they wished to roam, too. Iris wanted Anandra to do what she did best: she wanted her to take control of her body, of her mouth, her cunt, her breasts... and her mind.

"Undress for me. I want to watch you reveal your skin to my eyes. And do it slowly." Anandra walked over to the large, comforter-covered bed, never taking her eyes off her as Iris began to strip off her clothes as ordered, as slowly and sensually as she could manage. Iris had grown far more secure in her ability to arouse while she'd been in this world, and so Anandra's lascivious smirk didn't surprise her as it once would have. She loved that Anandra was playful when it came to sex, she loved the way she gazed at her as she undressed, like she was the most delicious, delightful thing Anandra had ever seen, and she loved the way Anandra threw her onto the bed, now, roughly, like she owned her, like she wanted her more than words could say.

Iris knew by now that words weren't necessary, anyway. She could make it clear to Anandra that she wanted her, too, and would let her own her, if only for this night. She was proud of herself for keeping quiet when Anandra sank her teeth into her upper chest, but she was unable to keep still. She was even less able to do so as Anandra's fingers found her clit, hard and ready to give her an orgasm at a moment's notice, after some pressure and, it seemed, some pain.

"Don't come yet," Anandra growled as she stopped biting Iris, because apparently she could tell how easy it would be now, after all these times together, to push her into a full, powerful climax.

Easy indeed, because Iris almost came from the pressure as Anandra dragged her finger across her clit's surface one last time. It would have taken only a little bit more of her touch, only seconds more, and then Iris could have come.

But apparently they were sticking to the usual rule, the one where Anandra got to come first. Now it was Iris's turn to watch her strip out of her clothes, each piece falling to the dark wooden floor as Anandra put on a show for her, her movements rough where Iris's had been gentle, and powerful where Iris's had been submissive.

"Flip over," Anandra said, once she was completely nude. "Lie on your stomach."

"Of course, yes." Iris rolled over, uncertain as to what would happen next.

"And now I want you to see if you can bring a strap-on into the room again, straight onto my body. One with a nice big...dildo, was it? And if it could in some way pleasure me while I thrust it into you, that would be most appreciated."

Iris shut her eyes. She remembered a type of dildo she'd

seen online once. It was held inside the person who was doing the fucking by their cunt's strength, a large bulb held tight by their aroused, clenching pussy, and she also remembered that it had a built-in vibrator. Maybe she could bring that one into this—

She heard a loud, sudden gasp behind her and what sounded like some quiet but aroused cursing. "This will do nicely," Anandra said. Her voice was full of satisfaction, as apparently she was pleased with what Iris had come up with.

Very pleased, because with a small growl of joy, Anandra leapt onto the bed at Iris's left side, making the bed shake a bit. Then she caused Iris to get much wetter, much more aroused, as she slowly raked her nails across Iris's ass. She shivered at the pain from Anandra's fingernails and shivered once again as Anandra lay on top of her, kissing her back as she squeezed her sides in tight, grasping pulses. "I hope you're ready, I hope you're nice and fucking wet. Are you, Iris?"

"Yes, yes, I am. Please, go ahead."

"I will, I will. Patience, my dear." Anandra moved her body slightly, and then Iris felt the pressure of the rigid, thick dildo begin to slide inside her, felt herself tighten around it, and then felt Anandra drive its length home. All the way in, so fast, so deep, and it felt far, far better than Iris could have predicted. Those beginning sensations of pleasure almost doubled in size when the dildo began to vibrate, causing both of them to gasp and then moan, Anandra's sound longer and louder than Iris's, since her clit was clearly experiencing the vibration, and Iris's wasn't.

She didn't mind, though, because the dildo was stroking her G-spot as it slid, so slowly, in and out of her. Stroking it damn good, just like Anandra was fucking her damn good, and she grinned into the pillow as each movement and thrust of the dildo slowly massaged her cunt. Anandra grabbed her wrists, pinning them down to the bed, and began to fuck her harder, faster, saying, "You're mine, you're all mine, Iris. I get to do whatever I want with you, don't I?"

"Yes, yes, ma'am, you do!" Iris squealed as Anandra began to slam the dildo into her, almost too rough in her fucking, just on the edge of being too rough...the very heavenly edge, the edge otherwise known as "perfection." It felt so perfect that Iris thought she was close to coming, even though Anandra was nowhere near her clit, not even close, although there was a slight pull at it each time Anandra spread her wide with a long, solid thrust of the dildo. She felt full, and close...full of silicone dick and close to coming, and then Anandra let out a yell, shaking above her and digging her nails into Iris's sides as she came.

"Fuck...fuck...fuck! Oh!" The last sound was long and drawn-out, and, Iris thought, incredibly hot.

And now it was her turn. Anandra reached down and began to play with her clit, a bit of a tease at first, edging around it and then sliding her fingers down to stroke other parts of her cunt, spreading its wetness around and causing Iris to make very grumpy noises every time her fingers traveled away from her clit.

"If you insist, I *guess* I could," Anandra said, and brought her fingers back to Iris's clit, using some of her apparently still-remaining energy, even there after that amazing-sounding orgasm, to fuck and rub Iris into one of her own. She tightened beneath Anandra, came as she bit down on the pillow beneath her head, and then she collapsed, lying very still and smiling softly with her eyes shut.

She felt Anandra rise from the bed. "Time for sleep, sweetness. We have a big day tomorrow, our biggest so far. A long trek to the castle and then we're getting you home. I hope you're looking forward to it."

Iris slowly opened her eyes. "Um, yeah, I…sure. I'll get off the bed now so we can get under the covers."

"That sounds good. Which side do you want?"

Iris was touched that she had asked, but she insisted that Anandra choose instead. They ended up with Anandra on the side nearest the door, a decision that Iris figured she hadn't made lightly. Anandra's watchfulness as they crawled into bed and got ready to sleep told Iris she was worried about Tressa, or at least didn't know how safe they would be while they slept. Iris still felt safe, though, lying here in the room of the house she didn't remember but still knew as home, its pervasive feeling of home-ness impossible to ignore.

The tension from worrying about Tressa gave her some trouble with falling asleep this night, and it seemed that Anandra had some difficulty as well. She was tossing and turning for almost as long as Iris lay there, awake and staring at the ceiling, wondering what everyone was up to back on Earth, and wondering if she'd be thinking the same thing about here, about Oria when she went home.

Home. What was home, really? Was it where the ones you loved lived? And if it was, where did that mean home was for Iris?

CHAPTER FOURTEEN

Iris guessed she'd been asleep for a fair number of hours when something woke her. Dawn was just breaking, the palest light coming in through their bedroom window, and she watched the sun rise for a few moments before she went downstairs to get a drink of water.

But halfway down the stairs, she saw an image appear at the bottom. It was a familiar image by now, and one that was very dear to her—Sallie stood down at the stairs' end with a smile on her face.

"Good to see you, pumpkin. I'm glad you're safe."

Iris hurried down the rest of the stairs, stopping right in front of her grandmother. "I know your real name now, you know."

Her grandmother winked at her. "Well, aren't you the smart one. Got anything else new to tell me?"

"I'm…I'm not sure I want to go home. Back to Earth, I mean. You're here, and Kahar is here, and…"

"And someone else who is dear to you is here, too…isn't she?"

"Fuck." Her grandmother had always been quick to figure things out, solving crosswords in record time and catching Iris the one time she stole something before they'd even left the store. "If you know, do you think she knows?"

"I couldn't say. I haven't seen enough of your friend to know if she might have noticed. But I am sure of one thing, and that's that you deserve her feeling the same way about you that you feel about her. You always were such a sweet child, kiddo. But I need to tell you something before you go get that glass of water."

"How did you...never mind. What is it?"

"I have been reading the future, like always, and I have seen Queen Tressa, waiting for you in her labyrinth. I have a feeling that you might end up there, and I also think that the message Anandra is delivering will seal your fate, that it will either stop Tressa or help her to win."

"But...win? What's she trying to do? And what does the message say?"

"I wish I knew, kiddo. I wish I knew. But I want you to know that I—"

Suddenly, her grandmother's face was gone, and instead, Iris saw a hazy image before her and watched as it became more and more defined. It was the woman from the previous day, Tressa, and she was talking to an old man. "The labyrinth is ready, then? It can hold them until I do what I've planned?" She was pacing back and forth, but each stride was confident, as was her face, almost as if she was certain her plans, whatever they were, would succeed.

"Wait," she said, pausing in midstep. "I sense someone. Who's there? Who's *there*?"

There was a quiet popping noise, and then the image was gone. Iris was shaking by the time it had disappeared, a chill coming over her that she wanted to get rid of as soon as possible. She rushed up the stairs and got back into bed, placing her head on Anandra's bare chest and using her body to warm herself. It seemed to work, her shivers fading quite quickly, but she was unable to sleep any longer, instead wondering what lay ahead of them for the rest of the day. She thought with a quiet smirk that, for a great fighter and protector, Anandra slept like a log and snored like a chainsaw at times, too. A ladylike chainsaw. She was snoring right then, even, a small smile on her face, and then she mumbled the word "Iris" softly, her smile growing wider.

"I love you, Anandra," Iris said under her breath, and Anandra sighed as she started to roll over in Iris's direction.

"Did you say something?" Anandra murmured against her cheek.

"Nothing, no. I was just thinking that we should probably get up now, because as you said, we have a long day ahead of us."

"Yes, Iris, we do." Anandra stretched her arms and legs, made a small grunting sound as she extended them, and then grabbed Iris up in her arms. "I have a good idea for how we can start the day, though…"

She began to kiss Iris and then seized her wrist, pulling the hand down to her own cunt. Iris took the hint, beginning to rub at Anandra's clit. She wanted to make this time count, because who knew how many more times she'd be able to lie in Anandra's arms, be able to kiss her or to get her off. Probably not many, maybe not even one more time. So this morning would really have to be good.

She got Anandra off once with her fingers, then crawled down her body and began to eat her out. And as she used her mouth, even less time passed before Anandra came for the second time. Then she picked up the dildo from the side of the bed, where it had been left after their last time together, and got Anandra off a third time by fucking her with it, nice and slow, while she worked her clit with her free hand. The fourth time she kissed Anandra and used her hand again, and then Anandra pinned her to the bed and ordered her to come as she worked at her cunt with both her hands. And Iris did, oh, she did! She was lucky this time, because she got to come not four, but five times. How could she possibly have imagined how very orgasmic she could be, before Anandra had entered into her life?

And how could she imagine life without her? But she had to go home. It was where she belonged, and this was not her home, no matter what she told herself. It could never be that.

She and Anandra got dressed, and Anandra took her hand right before they left the room to go downstairs. She looked almost as if she might have wanted to say something to Iris, but she just swallowed loudly and then, in a gruff tone, said, "Let's go. Maybe we can beg for some breakfast first. I bet your grandfather makes a good one."

He was awake and downstairs when they got there, sitting in the chair they'd plopped his passed-out body into the night before, and reading a thick, leather-bound book. "Ah, ladies, my granddaughter and her girlfriend, good morning to you. I have some sweet-and-spicy flatcakes in the kitchen, just waiting to be eaten, if you'll only do me the honor."

"We'll be glad to! Right, Anandra?"

"I must admit, I am more than a little hungry. I didn't sleep well last night."

"Your snoring said differently," Iris said under her breath.

Anandra didn't seem to hear her, already halfway through the kitchen's open door, but a quiet laugh came from the chair where Kahar sat.

"Your grandmother snored, too," he told her once Anandra was in the kitchen. "Made a dreadful racket, practically rattled the walls. She was full-of-body, but that's how I've always liked my women. You want your arms to be filled up when you hug your love, or at least *I* did. You and Anandra have almost nothing to hold on to. That's why I've been trying so hard to feed you two as much food as possible while you've been here."

"I think it's working, too! I probably gained at least a pound from that delicious dinner you cooked last night!"

"You'll need all the fuel you can get for the rest of your travels today, I believe. So you'll also have eggs, fruit salad, and some non-alcoholic cider, nice and piping hot, exactly the way I like it."

"And cheefen?" Iris was quick to ask.

"Ah, I don't touch the stuff…caffeine is bad for your health. Besides, I've never needed it, even with your grandmother's snoring. She always lulled me to sleep pretty fast, once I got used to it."

"The same is true of Anandra's snoring, actually." Iris briefly considered asking him if he could scare up even some stale, decades-old cheefen buried somewhere in his pantry, but then she realized that she was wide-awake, even despite her less-than-enough night's sleep. Was she excited to be so close to returning home? Or was this nerves, instead?

She decided it was probably nerves as she went into the kitchen, following a cinnamon-and-sugar scent all the way over to what looked like spiced pancakes. Some butter was melting over them, and some berry syrup sat in a large bowl with a ladle in front of the tall, yummy-smelling stack. She also saw a large bowl of mixed fruit salad, some fried eggs of unknown origin, and two steaming mugs of cider, which smelled like it would taste a hell of a lot better than the first cider she'd had in this world.

In a strange way, it felt like she'd been here longer than the small handful of days she'd spent traveling this world's lands.

And it felt like she'd known Anandra far longer than she had actually known her, too. Iris didn't think much of the idea of past lives, always having considered them a bunch of hogwash, but as she plated her food and began to eat, she wondered if they were something that actually existed in this world. She thought of asking Anandra, who was currently stuffing her face in a slightly adorable way, but then she realized she didn't want to know, because either way, the answer seemed likely to cause her disappointment.

They finished their food and walked back upstairs, packing their things for the last time before their imminent arrival at the castle, where hopefully Iris could find a way to return to Earth. Kahar had sounded doubtful the night before that such a way existed, almost like Anandra had been pulling her leg this whole time, leading her to the castle for some other reason. But it was obviously not the case, and besides, it was too late to wonder about her motives. They seemed clear enough. No way was Anandra that good an actress, no way at all. She seemed almost too honest by now, at least compared to how she'd started out—so much more open that it was a beautiful thing to Iris, as she thought about how much more comfortable Anandra had seemed to grow over their travels. She hoped that comfort in her own skin would remain with Anandra after she'd left this place, leaving her behind, behind and…alone.

Iris looked at Anandra's face for a few moments, taking in her beauty once more, which still hadn't lessened to Iris's eyes in the least. No, she'd only become more enjoyable to look at as the days had passed. Iris had a feeling that this would never change, no matter how many times she looked at her.

But whether the intense attraction Iris felt would remain… that would always be unknown to her, just as imagining what their future might have been would have to remain in her imagination.

After everything was packed, they went back downstairs and Iris said good-bye to Kahar. If only it didn't have to be forever, she thought as she smiled at his kind face. But it seemed that even if she'd wanted to stay, the last queen, Tressa, didn't want this world to be safe to her, and although she realized then that she wanted to stay, desperately, she wanted to live, too, and it seemed like there was only one way to guarantee that she survived. She had to go back to Earth, and once there, she would have to try accept that her old life—her *real* life—was good enough.

As she and Anandra began walking away from the once-more invisible inn, she thought that at least her return wouldn't hold a single second of pining after Jane; at least she'd gotten one really good thing she *could* take back with her. Or three, actually: her self-respect, her self-esteem, and the belief that she could possibly find happiness with the right woman, once she returned to her own world.

However, it seemed that she was staring at the lovely, practically perfect backside of that "right woman" right now. Anandra chose the moment after those thoughts went through Iris's mind to slow down, turning back to smile at her. The smile told her what she'd wanted to know, or at least she thought it did—it was a smile that said "I love you, Iris." And it looked like it might have said something else: "Please, don't leave. I couldn't bear it."

But Iris was clearly reading too much into what was merely a smile, and so she took a few quick steps to catch up to Anandra and pointed at what looked like a large, female-shaped statue next to the castle. "What's that?"

"That's Queen Tressa's likeness, and it's rumored that an impossible and dangerous labyrinth is inside it, the one you heard about earlier on our journey."

"Impossible *and* dangerous, huh? I bet you could get

through it with enough magical power." Iris almost told her what her grandmother had said about the labyrinth, and then she remembered what she'd told her about Anandra's message for the current Queen of the land. "Hey, what does your message to the Queen say, anyway?"

"As I may have already told you, I am forbidden to read it or even open it. It is for the Queen's eyes only and has a magical, personalized seal on it anyway, so I couldn't even open it if I wanted to. Not that I do."

"You aren't even a little bit curious? I am. I'm extremely curious, to be honest. And for all we know, it could be important for us to find out what it says, what with Tressa's return to this world."

"Possibly, but as I told you, I can't open it, nor am I supposed to."

"Then that will just have to be fine, I guess," Iris grumbled. She was feeling supremely grouchy for some reason, and her grouchiness didn't fade one bit during the entire time they walked toward the castle.

The already big-looking castle grew in size as they traveled in its direction, at least according to Iris's eyes, growing larger and larger with each passing hour. The statue grew in size as well, and Iris could now see that it was at least a third taller than the castle itself.

"That Tressa must have had some ego, building her statue even higher than the castle."

"Oh, *did* she. But she's gone now...or at least she was, I should say. Curses to whatever has allowed her to return!" Anandra spat on the ground, and this time, Iris couldn't blame her, now that she knew the whole story. Yes, she couldn't even blame her for doing the same thing to Anandra's friends' floor, although it still couldn't be considered good manners.

All these things she'd learned about Anandra, all of them

were running through Iris's head nonstop, and she realized something as they finally reached the castle's drawbridge, wide enough for a four-lane highway and beyond solid looking. It should have been obvious, she thought as she stepped onto the wide, wooden bridge. It should have been obvious—she was angry that she had to go home, and she was angry at Anandra for being okay with that. And more than anything, she was angry…no, pissed, royally pissed…that this Tressa bitch had to spoil any chance of her staying here.

She'd just have to make the best of these last however-many hours she had with Anandra, and if she was really lucky, she would get to spend some of them in her lover's…no, in her *love's* arms. It might make the pain worse, but she'd be able to remember Anandra's touch better that way. She'd be able to remember the exact feel of her curves against her body and to remember her scent, a scent full of the heady smell of the woods. Yes, she wanted to remember everything she could about the amazing woman who was using the silver knocker on the palace's large right-hand door, who was now turning to her with a slight, shy smile and saying, "It should only be a moment's wait."

"That's fine, I don't mind waiting." Iris would have accepted the longest wait possible, anything to drag out the time she had remaining in this world.

But they really had only a moment's wait, as a small window at the top of the door opened and a middle-aged man peered through its metal bars. "What business have you with the Queen?"

"I am Anandra of Basthar, and I come with a message for the Queen." Anandra reached into her bag and pulled out the sealed message, tilting it up toward the guard's face so he could see the seal, presumably.

"You may enter, then. I will see that you are escorted

to some temporary quarters while you wait for the Queen herself. It should be no more than two sun-falls or so." The small window was shut once more, and then Iris heard what sounded like something heavy and solid being moved, and the right-hand door swung open with a loud, steady screech accompanying its exceptionally slow movement.

"Welcome to Queen Yez's castle," said a curvaceous, blond woman in a long, pale-pink gown. She was very attractive, Iris thought, and so was her ample cleavage. Had it been magically enhanced? It was rather disproportionate. Not that she was about to complain about the free show or anything, although she did her very best to keep eye contact as the woman introduced herself and began to lead them down a huge stone hallway. "I am Keni, and I welcome you here. Refreshments will be delivered to your room, and we will ring the bell to wake you, should you need to rest after your lengthy journey. I hear that the Basthar territory is more than a day's travel from here."

"Much more than a day's travel," Anandra told Keni.

Iris looked around her as they followed Keni down the hallway. Tapestries hung from the walls at even intervals, showing many different creatures of the world and men and women wearing crowns. Would one of the women be her grandmother, with her grandfather next to her? Then, on one of the tapestries, she saw a woman with long brown hair who looked like her grandmother might have looked when she was much younger.

"Is that Queen Selehn?" she asked Keni.

"Yes, our good Queen Selehn. I was born after her reign, but Queen Yez has had nothing but wonderful things to say of her during the glorious sun-cycles of her rule."

Ah, apparently the help had to kiss up to the current Queen, because Keni didn't sound entirely like she meant it when she called the Queen's reign "glorious." However, Iris could have doubted the truth of her words because she was just fatigued from the day's long walk. They hadn't even stopped for lunch, and now she was either in desperate need of a nap or something to eat. "These refreshments, will they include food?"

"Of course, that can be arranged. Would you like a full meal? It is almost time for dinner, after all, although we eat later here than most do in our land, for the Queen's schedule is always very full. She manages it extremely well, though, exceptionally so, at least according to me."

They had taken two left turns while she and Keni had been talking, and now they'd reached a long, torch-lit hallway with very few windows. Keni stopped at the third door down and took out a key from her skirts, unlocking the door and swinging it wide open. "One of the Queen's butlers will get you some lovely food and drink very soon. Will you be wanting some alcohol?"

Iris felt like she needed it, but she wanted to stay as clear-headed as she could over the next two sun-falls, however long those happened to be. She wanted to experience her last hours with Anandra fully, without anything getting in the way of her choice to be as present as she could be. Nor did she want to have sex under the influence, if that was part of how they spent their final hours together. "No, thank you," she told Keni.

"The food will be delivered behind the small door to the left of the bed. It should take only a brief time for it to arrive, as I have already sent psychic word to the kitchen of what you will require."

"Psychic word?" Did that mean she was aware of Iris's thoughts about her breasts? And if so, was she insulted?

"They're real, by the way," Keni said, and laughed. "I'd let you feel them to prove it if you didn't already look so taken with the woman beside you. You're pretty cute, I must say." She giggled and then turned and trotted back the way she'd come, her laughter managing to travel down the hallway and straight into Iris's ears for longer than she might have liked.

"Now *that* was embarrassing!" Iris rushed into the room in an attempt to get away from the woman's wicked giggling as soon as she could.

"Embarrassing for you, entertaining for me." Anandra swatted her on the butt and swung the door shut behind her at the same time. "I think you should be punished for thinking such rude and dirty things. I also think you should be punished because I happen to believe you would have taken her up on her offer had you come here alone. You'd be groping her tits right now, perhaps rolling one of her nipples around in that pouting mouth of yours."

"I am not pouting." But Iris knew she was, and she also knew when she was beaten…but she knew when she wanted to be beaten sexually, too, and exactly where she wanted those strikes to land on her flesh. "Does that mean I'll be punished physically, then?" A small clanking sound came from their left, and Iris saw a bell swing back and forth next to a metal handle sticking out of the wall. "Never mind. Food first. As hard as it'll be to wait for you to punish me, I'll need all my strength to take whatever you give me, and I'm famished at the moment."

"I am as well. Let's see what this castle thinks is worthy to feed to commoners such as ourselves." Anandra walked over to the handle on the wall and pulled it, revealing that it was attached to a small, rectangular door that swung out into the room about a foot. Behind it was a large tray, holding two bejeweled glasses full to the brim with cherry-red liquid, a plate covered in grape-like fruit, cheese, and sliced white bread, and a second, smaller plate holding what looked like chocolate truffles. "Apparently they think well of commoners here. Shall we eat in the bed or at the table?"

The hallway leading to the room hadn't even begun to betray how fancy the rooms along it were, Iris thought, as she considered where to sit. This one held a bed, a large sitting room with a red-cushioned couch and matching chairs, and a door that probably led to the bathroom. The bed was a four-poster, with a red lace canopy, red satin sheets, a lace-edged, red comforter, and enough red satin, heavily tasseled pillows to fill up Iris's apartment back on Earth. "Who would need that many pillows? Is this an orgy room or something?"

"I bet you wish it was, based on what that psychic woman had to say." Anandra chuckled, but Iris shot her a look.

"You're the only one I wish was in here right now, just so you know. The only one." Iris knew she was pouting again, but she couldn't help it.

After sitting on the couch with Anandra and devouring over half of the food, though, she felt far less like pouting and was even smiling when Anandra reached up to her face and ran her fingers down her forehead, across her cheek, and then to her lips. Then she spread Iris's lips with her fingers, slowly opening her mouth with two fingers, then three, and then four. Iris did her best to suck on them, but her mouth was so full it was somewhat challenging. It was a challenge she was very pleased to accept.

At the same time her mouth was stuffed full of Anandra's fingers, Anandra began to talk dirty to her, making wetness begin to pool somewhere besides her mouth, her cunt growing moist and warm as Anandra spoke. "Do you like having your mouth spread wide, like a little slut?" she asked Iris. "Do you like having me take control of it, choosing what goes into it and how long it stays inside?"

Iris grunted in assent as best as she could manage with

her mouth so full, but Anandra seemed to understand what she was trying to say. "Good. Very good." She slowly pulled her fingers from Iris's mouth, sliding them down her face and letting some of her saliva moisten it as Anandra's fingers traveled over her chin and down her neck. She let her fingers linger between Iris's collarbones for a few moments, and Iris's pulse quickened. Her cunt began to pulse, too. Her clit was most likely hard as hell right then, just from these few subtle movements of Anandra's hand.

Anandra continued moving her hand down then, over the crevice between Iris's breasts, down and then up again, underneath her shirt. She shoved one cup of Iris's bra aside, grasping her breast in a tight and sudden squeeze of her fist. Iris swallowed hard, but she kept silent throughout the pain, and Anandra had a pleased expression on her face. Her stars even seemed to shine brighter. Good, this was doing it for her partner, too. She hoped Anandra was as wet as she was, as ready for things to continue heating up.

Anandra pulled her hand out of Iris's shirt then, letting go of her flesh, and Iris sighed at the sudden relief from the pain. "Too much?" Anandra asked, and Iris was quick to shake her head, quick to show Anandra that she could take it. And she knew she could take more, too.

"I'm good," she added.

"Yes, you are." Anandra's voice sounded remarkably gentle then, not at all like she was trying to take control, not at all like only moments before. Iris thought she saw Anandra's eyes get a little wet, and it looked like maybe she was fighting off tears.

But then Anandra cleared her throat, rising from the couch, and pointed to the bed. "Take off your clothes and get on the bed, but place your panties on it beside you."

Iris was quick to do as she was ordered, even though she

wanted to take her time, even though she wanted to make these last moments together take as long as possible. But her hunger for Anandra, for pleasing her, and for her own chances at coming overtook her hunger for lingering over this moment. Besides, as much as she wanted the sex to last, she wanted some time in Anandra's arms after they were done, because that was more important to Iris right then, even more important than following Anandra's orders. She would follow them, of course, because she'd found she loved to do so as much as she loved Anandra...or at least *close* to that second love's immeasurable amount.

"What now?" Iris asked. "What do you want me to do next?"

"I am overjoyed that you're so eager, Iris. I'll tell you what to do next," Anandra said, placing one steady foot after another in front of her as she rounded the couch and headed to the bed. "Next, I just want you to lie still and let me do as I wish."

"Of course, Anandra. I'll do anything you want, anything at all." Iris's breath caught in her throat for a second as Anandra reached the bed. She was just so striking a sight, with her white hair, which Iris now knew held some metallic glints in its shine, her luscious, dark skin, and the stars sprinkled generously across every inch of her. Iris had even noticed a few on her cunt's lips by now, and one happened to sit right on her clitoris. Iris chided herself for not paying enough attention to the stars' placement, for not memorizing where each and every one lay, and she realized now that she didn't even know if their glow had always brightened when Anandra was turned on, or if it just happened when Anandra was with her. She didn't really want to know the answer to that question, though, especially since now Anandra would have plenty of time to find other women who could make her stars glow the same way Iris had. To possibly make them glow brighter than they did with her.

"You know, my sweet, my stars have never shone as brightly as they do with you. It is strange…but not bad," Anandra added quickly, "not bad at all."

"Are you psychic now, too?" Iris joked, but underneath the joking was a feeling of relief that she had this special effect on Anandra. It was wonderful, knowing that she apparently did something for her friend that other women hadn't been able to. It was good to know this, but Iris only had a few seconds to linger on this revealing information before her mouth was suddenly stuffed full of the panties she'd placed on the bed. They were the second thing her mouth had been filled with in only a few minutes, and while she didn't mind them filling it up, she preferred Anandra's fingers. Because they belonged to her lover, of course, because they were part of her body.

Anandra climbed on top of Iris now and then shoved her legs open. "This time, since it will probably be our last, I will get *you* off first. And I demand that you come more than once."

Iris made what she hoped would come across as a sound of delight, but it was hard to communicate clearly around a mouthful of panties. Then other sounds came from her, ones that she knew communicated something else quite clearly: that she was melting against Anandra's tongue, as it slipped across her clit in its usually perfect fashion. It felt just as good as it always did, as it always had. But although Iris was trying to concentrate on Anandra's tongue on her clit, to fully feel her hands spreading her thighs wide, it took her a while to come back to this moment of pleasure. She didn't want it to end, and so when her orgasm began to climb, higher and higher, she pleaded throughout its body-quaking, shimmering intensity, pleaded with whoever or whatever guided this world to let her stay here with Anandra. To not allow this to be their last time together. To not make her have to choose between never seeing Anandra again and facing Tressa.

It was an impossible choice, a cruel one, but after her third orgasm had come and gone, and after the fourth one had finally swept her thoughts away from her future, she collapsed onto the bed and realized she still couldn't fully talk herself into staying. She was just too terrified of the evil ex-Queen. And what good was she to Anandra dead?

On top of that, she knew Anandra liked her, liked her a lot, but she had to be honest with herself: she didn't know if Anandra wanted her to stay. She had said no such thing, but when Anandra removed the panties from her mouth and frowned, Iris wondered if her unhappy expression and wet eyes earlier were her friend's way of telling her to stay. If Anandra asked, Iris couldn't possibly say no.

Instead of asking her to stay, Anandra asked her for an orgasm, and Iris gave one to her gladly. She was more than ready to give her a second one, but instead of allowing her to, Anandra changed position, moving her body down Iris's until their faces were almost touching. She stared into Iris's eyes for one long, intense moment, then placed her lips where her cunt had just been, kissing Iris deep and long. It was a tender kiss, much more tender than usual, but her frown returned as soon as she pulled back from Iris's face. "I would assume that our time is almost up. We should get dressed so we can look proper for the Queen. I'm not sure if I can get something nicer to wear out of my bag, and besides, I don't think royalty should get to see me in something more special than you've seen me in. But you will need some new panties."

Iris found herself smiling easily at Anandra's comment. Apparently she could still smile without too much trouble, but doing so would get a lot harder once she was gone from this land. Anandra drew some burgundy, lilac-trimmed panties from her bottomless bag, and they got dressed again in silence, barely looking at each other as they covered up each bit of skin. Iris knew her clothes from this world wouldn't blend in all that well on Earth, but hopefully she could somehow be sent back to somewhere more familiar than that field she'd woken up in. She still didn't know how she'd ended up there, nor did she know how she'd wound up in Oria, but she was almost positive by now that Tressa had something to do with it. Well, whatever Tressa's plans for her were, they weren't going to happen, because Iris would be long gone by the time Tressa was able to make her way to the castle.

Just as they finished dressing, a bell near the door rang four times, the sudden sharp sound making Iris jump a little.

"You aren't nervous, are you?" Anandra asked her. Iris shook her head. "Of course you are. All along, I told you that my tutor could get you home, and now your grandfather has planted the idea in your head that he won't be able to. I still believe he can, though, because my tutor was the best in the land for many sun-cycles, and may still be today, although I hadn't heard of your grandfather before I met you, and his powers…if he spoke the truth, of course."

"You're accusing my grandfather of lying? After all he did for us?" Iris almost placed her hands on her hips, but instead she stomped over to the room's door. "He's obviously trustworthy."

"Either that, or you are too trusting," Anandra said haughtily.

So this was how things between them were going to end. With a petty fight and some hard, mean words. It made Iris more comfortable than she had been about leaving, as they continued to argue, waiting to be led to the Queen's quarters. Iris slung her bag over her shoulder and crossed her arms, as she and Anandra ran out of things to say. That had never been a problem before, not even with Anandra's lack of interest in talking at the beginning of their journey. Even then, it hadn't been impossible to draw her out of her shell, and drawing her out of it had only become easier as they spent more time together. If Anandra wanted to climb back into her shell now, if she wanted to slam it shut, that was just fine by Iris.

A brief knock on their door came shortly, and Anandra said, "You may enter."

It was the same maid as before, Keni, but her assets did nothing for Iris this time around, nothing at all. She was too angry to feel sexual toward anyone, and she had no trouble at all keeping her eyes on the maid's face. "I will lead you to the Queen's quarters. She has been busy all day, preparing for war against Tressa's rebuilt armies."

"So it is true, then," Anandra said. "We ourselves have seen a woman who was called Tressa by someone we met, but I was not sure until now that it was truly her."

"You weren't?" Iris huffed at Anandra's words. She'd never experienced this kind of rudeness from Anandra. It was almost as bad as Jane had been, and she had no room in her life for another Jane. When they reached a large, open door, Anandra turned to Iris and said her name, once. She said it in a far kinder tone than she'd been using during their fight and walk down the castle's halls. "I'm…I'm sorry we have to part like this. I will be heading straight home as soon as my message is delivered and after I have contacted my tutor. He's a very busy man, but he's very curious, too, so he should be happy to make time for you very soon. I will arrange a place for you to stay here, I promise." Then she gestured to the open doorway. "Ladies first."

Iris found tears threatening to fall as she walked past Anandra, but she wasn't willing to let them. They would deliver this message and Anandra would be off, and maybe then, once she was gone, she would allow herself to cry. Anandra might have been cruel, but so had she, and their parting would have been painful no matter what treatment she received before she went home. She still didn't know if Anandra's tutor would even be successful, though, and she felt a slowly growing sense of fear threaten to outgrow her strong feelings of anger and sadness.

She could barely take in the room she had just entered, full as she was of intense thoughts and moods. She did notice the middle-aged woman on the lengthy couch, though, with silver and golden-blond hair flowing past her waist. The woman wore a crown and an anxious expression, her lips tight and her brows knitted together. She didn't look as if she'd even noticed the women entering her room, but then she turned to them, straightened her back, and spoke. "I hear you have a message for me?" she asked Anandra.

"Yes, Your Majesty, I do. Your cousin in Fehl sent me, and he told me to get it to you immediately."

"My cousin in Fehl?" The Queen sounded doubtful, almost like she didn't even remember she had a cousin there, but then she stretched out her hand. "Give it to me, please."

Anandra took the message from her bag and handed it to her, bowing slightly as the Queen took it.

Queen Yez whispered a few words and rubbed her hand over the message's seal, and Iris grew tense as the seal started to move off the message, undulating onto the Queen's dress. "Get it off me! Get it off!" She jumped up, trying to grab at it, but it still continued to travel across her skin. Then her eyes fell shut, but instead of falling into a faint, she smiled, a cruel smile that didn't seem to belong on her face.

"Good," she said. "It worked!" Her voice came out rough

and hard, nothing like how it had sounded before. It was almost as if it were someone other than her who was now speaking.

Iris turned to Anandra, who hadn't moved an inch, and she didn't look nearly scared enough, considering all that had just happened. But that was the last thing Iris could register before she saw a cloud of black smoke come rushing at her face from Queen Yez's direction. She would have screamed—oh, how she wanted to—but everything happened so fast she was only able to notice that she was falling backward, and she knew then that no one was going to catch her.

CHAPTER FIFTEEN

"Iris...Iris! Please, please be all right. I'm...I'm sorry for our fight. I just didn't want you to leave...I'm so sorry."

Iris barely managed to open her eyes. She had the headache to end all headaches, and a very worried-looking face was directly above hers. Anandra's. She was kneeling and looked close to tears, but Iris had to wonder if they were real tears or faked. After all, she thought as she pushed up and saw a possibly also faked look of relief rush across Anandra's face, everything that had happened, everything that had led her here, had been Anandra's doing. Maybe she was in cahoots with Tressa, because the area Iris was now lying in had a distinctly labyrinthine feel to it. She noticed with fear that the room had about four exits, probably all leading to eventual doom. Or maybe not even all that eventual.

"This is your fault, isn't it?" Iris grumbled, holding her head as she got up as quickly as she could manage. Her head spun a little from the effort, and Anandra reached forward to steady her. Iris allowed her to do so. After all, anything to put off her clearly oncoming death sentence, which Anandra had helped lead her straight to.

"I know you probably don't want to trust me right now," Anandra said, bowing her head.

"You're right, I don't."

"But I don't think you have a choice."

"Oh, *really*?" Iris let go of her head, taking in the room more fully now. She had been right—there were exactly four exits, all well lit, and after peeking into each of their doorways, she saw that they all split off after a number of feet. So, which one to take? It probably didn't matter in the end.

"You could always use this," Anandra told her. She reached into her shirt and pulled out a candle…and her knife. Iris flinched as its cold, deadly metal glinted in the room's torchlight, and Anandra seemed to notice, quickly lowering the hand that held it and sticking the knife partway into her pants' waistband.

"You managed to hold on to my grandfather's candle? Why would you do that if you didn't trust him?" Iris was getting more confused by the second, but at least her headache seemed to be fading as she tried to figure everything out. "And what was with the message you gave the Queen, anyway? Did you enchant it?"

"I didn't enchant it, no. To the best of my knowledge, her cousin sent it, although now I am starting to wonder if he was really her cousin or one of Tressa's henchmen. And I kept the candle because I figured it would come in handy, and I… maybe I lied about trusting your grandfather." Anandra looked away, biting her lip, then said, "Maybe I just wanted to be angry at you instead of…well, we should probably be on our way. Unless you have anything hidden on your person that can help us."

"No, I…wait." Iris now remembered the flower her grandmother had left with her, and she reached into her pants' pocket. It was still there, looking a little smooshed and worse for the wear, but completely intact.

"I know that flower! It…it…I think it can bring things to

you, if you wish on it. I'm not entirely positive, though. My tutor didn't spend much time on flowers."

"It's probably worth a try." Iris held it up to her face, shut her eyes tight, and searched for a wish. She found one almost instantly, a very clear picture of her grandmother popping into her mind.

"Where am I?"

Iris jumped, her eyes wide open now, and she spun around in the voice's direction. No, it couldn't be! "Sallie?"

"Yes, my dear," said her grandmother, "in the not-so-flesh. It's lovely to see you, of course, but how did I get here?"

"The flower you left me brought you. Thanks, by the way. I didn't know what it was until now."

"Flower? I may be old, but I'm not senile yet, and I never gave you a flower."

"Of course you did. It was just like the ones in your garden in this world, with the blue petals, and…" Iris looked down at her hand, to show the flower to Sallie, but it was gone. And now Sallie's words were sinking in. Shit! What had she done?

"We should make the best of a bad situation, pumpkin. I am at least grateful to get to see you again, although I must say, these are not the circumstances I would have hoped for." Her grandmother's projection had been glancing around the room after she'd appeared in it, and now she gave Iris a serious look. "It seems like you're in a bit of a pickle, Iris. If I didn't know any better, I'd think this was some sort of labyrinth. And if I still didn't know any better, I'd think it might be the one of legend that Tressa supposedly had built in her nasty likeness."

"I'm afraid you're probably right," Anandra said from behind Iris.

For once, Iris had completely forgotten Anandra was

there, since she'd been so startled—and overjoyed—by her grandmother's sudden appearance. "Sallie, this is Anandra. Anandra, this is Sallie or, as you might know her, Selehn."

"My good Queen, it is truly an honor to meet you. I think it's best if we save socializing for later, though, as I think we need to try to find a way out of here before Tressa finds us."

"She may already know where we are," Sallie said, "but there's no harm in trying to escape her grasp. I hope so, at least." She floated up to each of the doorways, peeking inside them. "My senses tell me we should take this one," she announced, pointing to the one farthest away from them.

"Senses?" Anandra asked.

"My grandmother has psychic powers."

"Ah, of course. Those must have been very helpful during the Great War."

"Sometimes yes, sometimes no. But I think they will be helpful now. Shall we, ladies?"

"I'll be happy to follow you," Iris told her grandmother. Anandra merely nodded in assent.

They started down the hallway Sallie had directed them to. Sallie went first, Iris second, and Anandra was the last to leave the room. Out of the corner of her eye, Iris saw Anandra draw her knife from her pants. She was hesitant about an armed Anandra walking right behind her, but she didn't really have a choice, and besides, if Anandra had been planning to kill her, wouldn't she have done it by now?

Sallie led them down passageway after passageway, pausing only a few seconds at each split in the tunnels before leading them in whatever happened to be her chosen direction. Iris was starting to wonder whether she knew what she was doing, but finally, it looked as if a bright light lay at the end of their current hallway. Was that the sun?

No, it wasn't. Instead, an exceptionally large room was

beyond that final hallway, lit by huge torches and full of statues. Very familiar-looking statues, Iris noticed at once. They were the same warriors she'd seen earlier on her travels with Anandra, the ones who worked for Tressa.

Yes, Tressa, who just happened to be sitting in a large, velvet-draped throne in the middle of the room. The warriors' cold eyes all moved toward them seconds after they entered the room, and Iris got ready to turn and run. But before she could, two warriors grabbed her and began to drag her straight to Tressa, a self-satisfied sneer spreading across her bloodred lips.

"My honored guests, at last we meet. Why don't you stay?" She cackled at her decidedly unfunny joke, and the warriors echoed her, the whole room filling with the sounds of their likely forced approval of her pathetic sense of humor.

Iris was feeling pretty pathetic right then, though, no longer in control of her feet or body. No, she wasn't in control of anything at all anymore.

She tried to fight the warriors who were dragging her along, but her strength couldn't even come close to matching theirs. And even if Anandra had a hundred of those stones from earlier, she wouldn't have enough time to use them all before she was stopped, for the warriors numbered in the hundreds, if not the thousands. Iris stopped struggling against the warriors, instead looking at Anandra and her grandmother for what would probably be the last time. Now Anandra was being dragged forward as well, and the warriors had wrapped some sort of magical rope around her grandmother's translucent wrists and were now dragging her along right behind Anandra.

When all three of them were lined up before Tressa, she rose from her throne and stared down at them. The scornful pride on her face showed that she knew she'd won. "Finally, Selehn, I have you on your knees. I knew your granddaughter was the only one who could wish you here. You don't know how long it took me to get back here, or how long it took me to build my army back up, but—"

"Actually, I do," her grandmother answered. "I'd guess about twenty sun-cycles or so."

"Silence. You are now within my grasp, finally, and you will obey me!" Tressa reached down and lifted a tall silver staff, topped with a red-eyed serpent. Its eyes began to glow, and Iris watched in terror as light shot out from them, hitting her grandmother's projection and quickly coating it with bright-red light. Her grandmother screamed for what seemed like a horribly long time, and then her head fell forward and the light disappeared.

Now her grandmother was flesh and blood, Iris could see. Now she was really in the room. Now, most likely, Tressa finally had what she wanted.

"You win, my old friend. Well played." Sallie's voice shook a little as she spoke, but her gaze was steady as she looked up at Tressa's face. "What will you do now?"

"Take over the land, of course. My armies have already begun, and as we all know, you are the only one who could possibly stand in my way. But I did not know where you were, and I knew I could not use the wishing flower to find you. Only one who has a stupid, kind heart can use those flowers, as we all know. Now, it is time for you to die, Selehn, but first, I will take the life of your daughter's special friend."

While Tressa had been speaking, Anandra had managed to get her arm out of the warrior's grasp, and now she slipped something into Iris's hand. It was cool and slightly thick, and Iris saw it was her grandfather's candle. But how would she light it, with her arms held so tight? And even if she could get free, what would she light it with?

Her first question was answered when Anandra fought the

warrior's other hand off her, and Iris watched as she stabbed one in the throat and sliced the other one's head clean off. But just as quickly as its head had disappeared, another one grew back.

Her plan had worked, though, because now the warriors who had been holding Iris let go of her and began to grab at Anandra, who managed to just barely escape their large fists each time they tried to strike her.

Now it was up to Iris, entirely up to her. "Fuck," she swore, "what am I supposed to do now?"

"You'll figure it out," Anandra yelled. "I know you're smart enough to." This time one of the warriors' hands made contact, and Anandra doubled over as it hit. "Use your powers," she groaned, and then she fell to her knees.

Her powers. Of course! Could she use them in such a tense situation, though? One where the tension didn't come from arousal but instead a rather large amount of terror? Could she do this?

Iris screwed her eyes shut tight, praying that she could, and then she felt a light weight inside her till-then empty hand. She opened her eyes and looked at what that hand held. A long match, red-tipped and made of dark wood, lay there in her palm. Time for some famous last words, she thought, and she struck the match on the stone floor, bringing it to the candle's wick.

"Please, please, light," she begged, her words sounding much like the ones Anandra had said when Iris had come to. Anandra, who now had her arms bent behind her back, her head held in place by one of the warriors. Anandra, who probably didn't have long to live. Anandra, who was now saying something, just as the candle's wick began to burn.

"If I don't make it," Anandra said, then groaned. Her voice was weak but empty of fear. "If I don't make it, I want

you to know that my last thoughts will be of you, sweet Iris…
my love."

But before the warriors could deliver the killing blow,
all four of them stumbled backward at the same time. Was it
working? Iris looked around, watching as the warriors closest
to them began to look strange around the tops of their heads,
almost like they were…melting?

Yes, they were! First, the crowns of the warriors' heads
turned to liquid, running down their faces, past their eyes, eyes
that were also melting now, and soon their lower heads melted,
too. Next, their shoulders became soft, and then their arms,
and soon enough, only a puddle remained where each warrior
had once stood.

And Iris now stood up, holding the candle firmly in her
hand as she rose. No *way* was she going to let go of it any
time soon. No, she wouldn't loosen her hold on the wonderful
magic candle until it had done everything it needed to do.

As the warriors who had been restraining her grandmother
also stumbled back and began to melt, she heard Tressa's now-
frightened voice call out. "No, warriors, seize them! Do my
bidding! You…you must! No!" As she became more and more
helpless, her voice filled with more and more fear, warrior
after warrior melting into a puddle of useless liquid.

Useless to Tressa, at least, but very useful to Iris and
Anandra and, of course, Sallie. Or Selehn, as she might call
her instead. Iris knew she could never get used to calling her
grandmother that name, any more than she could get used to
this world. Or could she?

Iris watched now as Tressa's staff melted, just as the
warriors had. And then sparks started raining down from the
ceiling, right above Tressa, hitting her throne and her head
and shoulders. They fell faster and faster, soon just a blur of
bright fire, until Tressa was completely enveloped in their

reddish-orange glow. She opened her mouth wide and began to yell something, but she couldn't get a single sound out of her mouth, because with one last, gigantic circle of fire falling from above her, a huge flash of light spread from where she stood, and when it had faded, she was gone, only a pile of smoking ash remaining where she had once stood.

Iris's task was clearly done, the large room now filled with dark, oily-looking puddles. She now had time to think for the first time in hours. Did she really want to return home? Or had this new world, full of epic magic, awe-inspiring creatures, and an awe-inspiring woman, become her new home? True, she had friends back on Earth, and her foster parents were there, too—she would have to figure out some kind of way to still see them, of course.

Wait. Was she *really* considering this? Was she actually thinking of staying here?

But then her grandmother turned to her, a bright grin lighting up her beautiful face, and her next words were all the answer Iris needed to help her make up her mind. "I think someone is waiting for the three of us outside. Two someones, actually...I think it's your parents, and I think they're waiting to see you. Yes! They are! Follow me, ladies, follow me!"

Her grandmother took off at a rather fast run for a woman her age, but Iris didn't have time to wonder how a woman who'd said she needed a cane could book it like that. Instead, she turned to Anandra and held out her hand. "Are you coming with us?" she asked.

She didn't have to wait long for an answer. Anandra took Iris's hand in hers, held it to her lips, and then kissed it. "That's the easiest question I've ever been asked."

"Easiest? What do you mean? Is that a 'yes'?" Iris kept her eyes on Anandra's face, wondering what her words meant.

"It means yes. Yes, I most definitely am."

They hugged each other for a few seconds, and then the words that Iris had whispered to Anandra the night before were now whispered back. "I love you, Iris. Please stay. Please. Now that you're safe."

"I most definitely will," she answered, and Anandra laughed.

"You silly lathron!"

"Lathron?" Iris asked.

Anandra began to walk toward a brand-new door where sunlight lit the outdoors in a most splendid way. It lit up Anandra's stars, too, and Iris took in their sparkling light, her eyes dancing across Anandra's skin before they settled on her face. "Lathron are a type of bird. They repeat back whatever they hear. You still have much to learn about this world, my dear. And I will be happy to teach it all to you. Now, do you want to see your parents, or not?"

"Yes, I do, I really do! And I want them to meet you, too. What should I tell them? What should I call you when I introduce you?"

"Anandra the Great, Slayer of Beasts. And hearts." She winked at Iris, and her stars shone brighter still. Iris knew that, in that moment, it wasn't the sun that was making them glow so brightly.

It was her.

Loved

Out of This World?

Now fall

Under Her Spell

Turn the page for a preview of
Under Her Spell
by Maggie Morton

Available now from Bold Strokes Books

Terra glanced out her window again, seeing the moon was still full but a bit higher in the sky. Where was she? Athene was almost never late for their rendezvous, as punctuality was one of her many, many loveable traits. What could be keeping her?

But then Terra heard a soft knock on her door, and it slowly opened, and Athene entered the room on quiet, slippered feet.

"Are the bunny slippers new?" Terra asked.

"They were a regrettable gift from my aunt. She's visiting right now, so I've been wearing them around in the morning and at night. That's not the worst part, though."

"No? You mean something like hot-pink and lime-green striped bunny slippers with psychotic-looking googly eyes can get worse?"

"Yes," Athene said, easing herself down onto Terra's quilt-covered bed. "They used to squeak."

Terra laughed at that, then cleared her throat. "You poor thing. But...what do you mean 'used to'?"

"I kind of let Onyx chew on them last night—his idea, not mine. That cat is part devil, I sometimes think, but he's still helpful in my spells."

"I need more than a super-attentive familiar to help with mine," Terra said, not without a hint of disappointment in her tone.

Athene sighed, reaching out for Terra's hands and pulling her onto the bed to her right. "If only your mother..."

Then Terra let her face fall, her lips turning down into a sad pout. She had intended to use those lips for kissing tonight, and not much more. After all, it was their second-to-last night together before the goddamned quest, and they'd already said everything there was to say. About how they'd miss each other. About how worried they were about Terra's chances, since she had so little power, power that could have been practically immeasurable if it hadn't been for her mother...but no, Terra decided. Tonight was not for worries or sad thoughts about the past.

"I'd rather kiss you now than start crying," Terra said, her voice soft.

"Me too, my love." Athene cupped the back of Terra's head, her fingers flowing through Terra's short-cropped curls, their striking blue-black the first thing Athene had noticed about her—as she'd told Terra the first time they were alone and able to talk. That talk had led to late-night meetings in Terra's quarters, late-night meetings that led to amazing sex, and, after a while, amazing love.

Their first time together had not been the first time either of them had gone to bed with a woman, but it had been the first time Athene had come while in someone else's arms. She was amazed, she had told Terra, amazed at how well Terra's hands had worked her body...her *flesh*. And Terra, in turn, had been amazed at how aroused Athene had become, with only a few kisses against each breast, her hand buried between Athene's thighs—a hand that had gotten soaked in seconds, Athene's wetness dripping down those thighs as they kissed and touched and moaned, Terra whispering dirty things into Athene's ear as she worked her clit.

Maybe it was her words (Athene later told her no one had ever talked dirty to her before). Maybe it was the excitement and Terra's immense desire for her (she'd only had sex twice before, with two different—and, as she told Terra, seemingly disinterested—partners). And maybe they just had some sort of magical chemistry on that night, because Athene got Terra to come, too, her mouth tight on Terra's cunt, as Terra continued to talk dirty to her, growling word after word about how naughty she was, and how dirty she was, bedding down with one of the staff, one of the people who was normally far below her, and now *she* was the one servicing Terra, instead of the other way around.

After they'd both come an equal number of times, Athene turned to face Terra, a very serious look on her face. In an equally serious tone of voice, she'd told Terra that she didn't look at the staff the way Terra thought she did, and that while it had been hot while she'd been eating her out, "You shouldn't assume that I look down on you normally. You're far too beautiful for that, for one thing." Terra had turned her head down, a flush rising to her throat and cheeks, and Athene had told her she looked exceptionally cute when she blushed.

Terra was desperate to see her again after that, and the desperation was returned in kind, because that night turned into a long trail of nights, turning into over a year of amazing—but private—romance. And it came with many, many more nights just as hot as that first encounter.

But tonight would just be sex, because the love part was too painful. After all, Terra thought, as she began to unlace the front of Athene's silk nightgown, tonight would be their last night together for…well, best not to think about that. What an arousal killer, worrying about missing each other. No, instead, she chose to take in Athene's chest as her nightgown slipped off her breasts—breasts she couldn't find a single flaw in. Just like Athene's face, its shape narrow and delicate, with equally delicate features and the most kissable lips imaginable. Lips that she was kissing right now, kissing with a hunger she hadn't expected to have. She felt ravenous, starved for contact, her desire mounting so intensely it almost drew the breath out of her. And then, when Athene took her hand and placed it on her right breast, the breath *was* drawn out of her, a quick, loud, exhale of warm air, warm air that made Athene shiver as it hit her skin.

Or perhaps the shiver came from the feel of Terra's fingers on her nipple, gently twisting it back and forth, the nipple hard with arousal, arousal that Terra knew had spread down to her lower parts as well. She knew this from the way Athene began to squirm a little as she tweaked her nipple, which she did a little rougher than usual, but her roughness didn't get any complaints out of Athene. No, instead she got a gasp, and a soft, "Please…"

"'Please' what, my girl?" Terra was grinning now, loving the power she had, able to turn Athene on so easily. It had always been like that, unlike any of the women she'd been with before their first night together. And now, a year and a half in, nothing had changed. At least, nothing when it came to the sex they had. Their sexual experiences hadn't dimmed a bit. The orgasms, and everything else, had only gotten better.

"Please…please, I want you to be rough with me tonight."

"Sounds good to me." Only a little time passed before she grabbed both of Athene's wrists and slammed her to the bed. "So, you want to be my slut tonight? My whore? Is that what you want?"

"I've been reading some books, books with stuff like this in it, and they really, *really* turned me on." Athene looked down shyly when she said this, but with a fair bit of excitement on her face as well.

"You sly little coquette! You slutty little bibliophile!" Terra chuckled, a low laugh that seemed to hold an unusual touch of darkness in it. "Just say 'warlock' if I get too rough. The thought of a man should turn both of us off right away. Just say that and I'll stop." Then she sunk her teeth into

Athene's shoulder. She didn't use an especially small amount of pressure. It was a test, to see exactly how much Athene could take and whether those books really did it for her as much as Terra hoped.

But Athene took it like a champ. She did shriek a little as Terra bit her, but it was a quiet shriek, and she said, "Thank you, mistress," as Terra loosened her mouth and then stopped. She didn't thank her when Terra bit her again, this time on the top of her left breast, this time a little harder. But Athene gave her the gift of a moan, because as Terra closed her teeth around her flesh, she also took her hands off Athene's wrists and started to grind her palm against her crotch. Terra's hand got incredibly wet as it worked away against Athene's panties, panties that were soaked through in an impressively short amount of time.

"You seem to like this, my lovely bottom."

"Yes, I must. I…I think I, um, more than just like it."

"That's good, because I really, really, really like it, too." As she growled each of those last six words, she ground her hand against Athene's panties, and when she finished her sentence, she slipped her hand inside them, finding that this was one fucking wet cunt.

"Goddamn, Athene, are you ever wet! You've *never* been this wet before. Seems like we've learned something new about you tonight." She slid her fingers down Athene's slit, finding a larger-than-usual clit in its certainly usual spot, and she began to rub it with her middle finger. With her other hand, she braided her fingers through Athene's long, full, golden hair, softer than silk and definitely far more beautiful. But she wasn't going to admire Athene's hair tonight, or compliment her in any way, unless it was to tell her how well-behaved she was, and how good she was at getting wet, and how pleasing it was to have such a submissive slut bottoming to her.

No, tonight Athene's hair was only a tool, one with which

to control her. Terra did just that, grasping most of it in a tight fist and then yanking it back, hard, as she added another finger to Athene's clit.

Athene had already been moaning a little, but now she was getting louder and louder. Terra noticed that she looked nervous, too. "I'm worried that I'll get too…fuck! Too loud! Oh, God, I'm going to get so loud, so loud. Oh, I'm close, Terra, I'm close."

"Are you going to come for me, my little bitch? Am I going to steal an orgasm or two from that sopping-wet cunt of yours?" She couldn't help but be slightly surprised at the words that were coming out of her mouth, and how easily they were coming to her. They'd never done anything like this before. It had always been gentle until then—lovely, and very, very hot, but there had been no hair pulling, no biting, and only a small amount of name-calling.

But at the last second, Athene threw up her arms, and a bubble of light suddenly surrounded the bed. Terra realized then that Athene had almost never come that hard. Nor was she often this loud, her cries echoing off the glowing circle of light around them. And as Athene came, Terra's heart began to beat hard, because she almost couldn't stand how beautiful Athene looked in that moment of ecstasy.

Fuck, she thought. *Fuck, I'm going to miss her too much.* How was she supposed to get through the next however-many-days this stupid, goddamn, sucky quest would take? It was all for the best prize in the world, though, the best prize imaginable—Athene's hand in marriage.

It was Terra's turn next, and Athene's gentle touch—with just the right amount of pressure in just the right places, and especially at just the right times—drew all thoughts of the next day out of Terra's head, and she worried less and less each time she came.

But soon—far too soon, in her opinion—it was time for her lover to leave. Not just her lover, no, because very few people will risk their lives for someone they just enjoy falling into bed with. No, there was much more to their relationship than that. Far more, because as Athene kissed her good-bye, she took Terra's hand in hers, and when she released it, a glowing, ghostly band was wrapped around Terra's left ring finger.

"How sweet!" She smiled widely and thanked Athene as she quietly opened the bedroom's door and shut it slowly behind her. Sadly, it was time for them to both try to get some rest before the next day.

But after Athene left, and once she was back in bed, ready to sleep, Terra waved her hand over the ring, making it turn into mist and then disappear. It was too sad, however sweet Athene's gesture had been, to see a ring on that finger, a ring that might never appear for real. She still had just a little hope that she would be successful, that her disguise would work the next night and that not only would she be allowed to compete, but that she would win. One of her last thoughts before she drifted under was one of hope.

Magic, even the most powerful in the world, should never even try to match the magic of true love. But was she right?

About the Author

Maggie Morton lives in Northern California with her partner and their two cats. She is the author of *Dreaming of Her*, winner of an Alice B. Awards Lavender Certificate, and *Under Her Spell*. Contact her at otterprawn@gmail.com.

Books Available From Bold Strokes Books

Let the Lover Be by Sheree Greer. Kiana Lewis, a functional alcoholic on the verge of destruction, finally faces the demons of her past while finding love and earning redemption in New Orleans. (978-1-62639-077-5)

Blindsided by Karis Walsh. Blindsided by love, guide dog trainer Lenae McIntyre and media personality Cara Bradley learn to trust what they see with their hearts. (978-1-62639-078-2)

About Face by VK Powell. Forensic artist Macy Sheridan and Detective Leigh Monroe work on a case that has troubled them both for years, but they're hampered by the past and their unlikely yet undeniable attraction. (978-1-62639-079-9)

Blackstone by Shea Godfrey. For Darry and Jessa, the chance at a life of freedom is stolen by the arrival of war and an ancient prophecy that just might destroy their love. (978-1-62639-080-5)

Out of This World by Maggie Morton. Iris decided to cross an ocean to get over her ex. But instead, she ends up traveling much farther, all the way to another world. Once she's there, only a mysterious, sexy, and magical woman can help her return home. (978-1-62639-083-6)

Kiss The Girl by Melissa Brayden. Sleeping with the enemy has never been so complicated. Brooklyn Campbell and Jessica Lennox face off in love and advertising in fast-paced New York City. (978-1-62639-071-3)

Taking Fire: A First Responders Novel by Radclyffe. Hunted by extremists and under siege by nature's most virulent weapons, Navy medic Max de Milles and Red Cross worker Rachel Winslow join forces to survive and discover something far more lasting. (978-1-62639-072-0)

First Tango in Paris by Shelley Thrasher. When French law student Eva Laroche meets American call girl Brigitte Green in 1970s Paris, they have no idea how their pasts and futures will intersect. (978-1-62639-073-7)

The War Within by Yolanda Wallace. Army nurse Meredith Moser went to Vietnam in 1967 looking to help those in need; she didn't expect to meet the love of her life along the way. (978-1-62639-074-4)

Desire at Dawn by Fiona Zedde. For Kylie, love had always come armed with sharp teeth and claws. But with the human, Olivia, she bares her vampire heart for the very first time, sharing passion, lust, and a tenderness she'd never dared dreamed of before. (978-1-62639-064-5)

Visions by Larkin Rose. Sometimes the mysteries of love reveal themselves when you least expect it. Other times they hide behind a black satin mask. Can Paige unveil her masked stranger this time? (978-1-62639-065-2)

All In by Nell Stark. Internet poker champion Annie Navarro loses everything when the Feds shut down online gambling, and she turns to experienced casino host Vesper Blake for advice—but can Nova convince Vesper to take a gamble on romance? (978-1-62639-066-9)

Vermillion Justice by Sheri Lewis Wohl. What's a vampire to do when Dracula is no longer just a character in a novel? (978-1-62639-067-6)

Switchblade by Carsen Taite. Lines were meant to be crossed. Third in the Luca Bennett Bounty Hunter Series. (978-1-62639-058-4)

Nightingale by Andrea Bramhall. Culture, faith, and duty conspire to tear two young lovers apart, yet fate seems to have different plans for them both. (978-1-62639-059-1)

No Boundaries by Donna K. Ford. A chance meeting and a nightmare from the past threaten more than Andi Massey's solitude as she and Gwen Palmer struggle to understand the complexity of love without boundaries. (978-1-62639-060-7)

Timeless by Rachel Spangler. When Stevie Geller returns to her hometown, will she do things differently the second time around or will she be in such a hurry to leave her past that she misses out on a better future? (978-1-62639-050-8)

Second to None by L.T. Marie. Can a physical therapist and a custom motorcycle designer conquer their pasts and build a future with one another? (978-1-62639-051-5)

Seneca Falls by Jesse Thoma. Together, two women discover love truly can conquer all evil. (978-1-62639-052-2)

A Kingdom Lost by Barbara Ann Wright. Without knowing each other's fates, Princess Katya and her consort Starbride seek to reclaim their kingdom from the magic-wielding madman who seized the throne and is murdering their people. (978-1-62639-053-9)

Season of the Wolf by Robin Summers. Two women running from their pasts are thrust together by an unimaginable evil. Can they overcome the horrors that haunt them in time to save each other? (978-1-62639-043-0)

The Heat of Angels by Lisa Girolami. Fires burn in more than one place in Los Angeles. (978-1-62639-042-3)

Desperate Measures by P. J. Trebelhorn. Homicide detective Kay Griffith and contractor Brenda Jansen meet amidst turmoil neither of them is aware of until murder suspect Tommy Rayne makes his move to exact revenge on Kay. (978-1-62639-044-7)

The Magic Hunt by L.L. Raand. With her Pack being hunted by human extremists and beset by enemies masquerading as friends, can Sylvan protect them and her mate, or will she succumb to the feral rage that threatens to turn her rogue, destroying them all? A Midnight Hunters novel. (978-1-62639-045-4)

Wingspan by Karis Walsh. Wildlife biologist Bailey Chase is content to live at the wild bird sanctuary she has created on Washington's Olympic Peninsula until she is lured beyond the safety of isolation by architect Kendall Pearson. (978-1-60282-983-1)

Night Bound by Winter Pennington. Kass struggles to keep her head, her heart, and her relationships in order. She's still having a difficult time accepting being an Alpha female—but her wolf is certain of what she wants and she's intent on securing her power. (978-1-60282-984-8)

Windigo Thrall by Cate Culpepper. Six women trapped in a mountain cabin by a blizzard, stalked by an ancient cannibal demon bent on stealing their sanity—and their lives. (978-1-60282-950-3)

The Blush Factor by Gun Brooke. Ice-cold business tycoon Eleanor Ashcroft only cares about the three Ps—Power, Profit, and Prosperity—until young Addison Garr makes her doubt both that and the state of her frostbitten heart. (978-1-60282-985-5)

Smoke and Fire by Julie Cannon. Oil and water, passion and desire, a combustible combination. Can two women fight the fire that draws them together and threatens to keep them apart? (978-1-60282-977-0)

Slash and Burn by Valerie Bronwen. The murder of a roundly despised author at an LGBT writers' conference in New Orleans turns Winter Lovelace's relaxing weekend hobnobbing with her peers into a nightmare of suspense—especially when her ex turns up. (978-1-60282-986-2)

The Quickening: A Sisters of Spirits novel by Yvonne Heidt. Ghosts, visions, and demons are all in a day's work for Tiffany. But when Kat asks for help on a serial killer case, life takes on another dimension altogether. (978-1-60282-975-6)

Love and Devotion by Jove Belle. KC Hall trips her way through life, stumbling into an affair with a married bombshell twice her age. Thankfully, her best friend, Emma Reynolds, is there to show her the true meaning of Love and Devotion. (978-1-60282-965-7)

Rush by Carsen Taite. Murder, secrets, and romance combine to create the ultimate rush. (978-1-60282-966-4)

The Shoal of Time by J.M. Redmann. It sounded too easy. Micky Knight is reluctant to take the case because the easy ones often turn into the hard ones, and the hard ones turn into the dangerous ones. In this one, easy turns hard without warning. (978-1-60282-967-1)

In Between by Jane Hoppen. At the age of 14, Sophie Schmidt discovers that she was born an intersexual baby and sets off on a journey to find her place in a world that denies her true existence. (978-1-60282-968-8)

Under Her Spell by Maggie Morton. The magic of love brought Terra and Athene together, but now a magical quest stands between them— a quest for Athene's hand in marriage. Will their passion keep them together, or will stronger magic tear them apart? (978-1-60282-973-2)